I0579836

秘 TRAPPED

Other Mei-hua Adventures

Hidden
A Mei-hua Adventure

Lotus Shoes
A Short Story from Ancient China

Warned
A Mei-hua Adventure

To discover more stories
about ancient China visit

padevoe.com.

A Mei-hua Adventure

P.A. De Voe

First Edition. First Printing, 2016

Printed in the United States of America

Publisher's Note
This is a work of fiction. Names, characters, places, and incidents either are the product of the author's imagination or are used fictitiously, and any resemblance to actual persons, living or dead, business establishments, events, or locales is entirely coincidental.

Cover design by Kelly Cochran

Published by
Drum Tower Press, LLC
165 Bon Chateau Drive
Saint Louis, Missouri 63141-6081
http://padevoe.com/?page_id=177

ISBN-10: 1-942667-04-3
ISBN-13: 978-1-942667-04-9

DEDICATION

To my readers.

Primary Characters

Trapped is set in 1380 China at the beginning of the Ming Dynasty. The characters below are listed with their family names first, which is the traditional Chinese system: family name then given name.

Zhang Mei-hua	Our heroine; temporary ward of Master Hsu and Madam Wu
Hsu Ping-an	Mei-hua's friend; daughter of Master Hsu and Madam Wu
Hsu Guei-lung	Ping-an's brother
Master Hsu	Ping-an and Guei-lung's father; Magistrate of the District
Madam Wu	Ping-an and Guei-lung's mother; Master Hsu's wife
Soldier Guo	Mei-hua's guard
Lord Chiu	Powerful eunuch
Da-shan	Former ruffian, now a Buddhist monk
Ching Da	Leader of gang
Aunt Xi	Ping-an's aunt
Gran'ma Fei	Madam Wu's brother-in-law's mother
Lotus Blossom	Mei-hua's maid
Orchid	Ping-an's senior maid

Chapter 1

MEI-HUA WAITED OUTSIDE Judge Hsu's office suite. She rocked from one foot to the other, wondering why he wanted to see her. Although she lived within his household, she hadn't seen him for several days. This was not unusual, since as magistrate for the district, he and his family all lived in the *yamen*, the official, governmental residence. The compound contained not only a private living area, but also the public spaces of the judge's official office, the judicial court, and the jail. Their paths didn't normally cross because the judge worked long hours and seldom visited the women's quarters where she lived with his daughter, Ping-an.

She scanned his door. A murmur of indistinct voices flowed steadily from his office. They wrapped around her, providing a constant background noise punctuated with intermittent hammering. She glanced around the courtyard and spied a carpenter repairing a wood lattice window shutter. A compound of this size always needed repair, she thought.

She mulled over the amazing number of people required to keep the yamen in good condition. Workers came and went continuously. She momentarily remembered how a mason happened to be near when Ping-an almost drowned. Having so many workers around had proved to be critical in saving her friend.

An approaching guard interrupted her reverie.

"Zhang Mei-hua, follow me," he commanded flatly before turning away. His clothing flapped against his boots as he strode back toward the office. Mei-hua rushed to keep up.

As she entered the official area, a massive, brightly painted *Xie Zhi* greeted her. With a dragon head, horn of a stag, back of a lion, scales of a snake, and tail of an ox, the statue announced to all who entered that this was the seat of justice. Its fierce eyes penetrated deeply, ferreting out truth.

She hoped the Xie Zhi would help them. The last time Mei-hua stood under the scrutiny of the Xie Zhi in this room was when she discovered Judge Hsu and her father had been fellow classmates and remained as close as brothers. Because of this long-standing tie, Judge Hsu took her into his family as his niece. Even more important to Mei-hua, however, was the judge's commitment to protecting and supporting her father in his struggle against an unseen enemy.

She stopped just within the room's entrance and, while clasping her hands in front of her, she formally bowed three times before the judge. He waved the members of his staff away.

"Come forward, Mei-hua," he said, once they were alone.

She approached his massive, ornately carved desk.

"I have heard from your father."

Mei-hua bent forward, a torrent of questions ready to spill out. Hsu stopped her with a raised hand.

"He's fine. He's still working as magistrate in Changsha district and holding court every day."

She unconsciously put a hand to her chest to feel for the jade amulet her father had given her and felt the smooth stone against her skin. In the past, as she struggled to find safety with her father's friend, the amulet had alerted her to the threat of danger. Now, its coolness reassured her.

Hsu went on. "That suggests his enemies haven't been able to pin the treasonous acts on him. Yet. It could also suggest...." He paused and stared at Mei-hua for a few seconds. She let her own gaze rest on his chin, for to look him in the eye would be a sign of disrespect.

He went on, "It could also suggest there is another plan being developed or perhaps already in the making. At this point, it's impossible to tell."

Mei-hua breathed deeply. The surrounding sounds of daily life stopped. The heat in the room rose to a suffocating level. Was he saying her father was safe or not safe? Were they no longer in danger or were they in greater danger? She stepped back to gain composure.

Judge Hsu watched her closely. "I want you to know these things because they impact you directly. Listen carefully."

Mei-hua's head spun; her silk tunic suddenly felt clammy and clung to her. Unable to speak, she silently bowed.

"Good. Let me start at the beginning. Your father sent you to me because he wanted me to protect you in case he was found guilty of treason. Our new Emperor, in his wisdom, has established the beneficent Ming Dynasty. However, he is troubled by enemies who want to bring down his dynasty before it has had a chance to be established. Therefore, he and his trusted servants relentlessly hunt down any person who *might* want to destroy his authority." He paused again before continuing. "I stress the word 'might' because clear evidence of treason isn't needed to condemn an official. Even the implication of possible treasonous behavior can be enough." He sighed.

"This makes it very easy for unscrupulous people to use the government's power in their personal vendettas against their own adversaries in order to destroy them." Shaking his head, he went on, "I believe this is what is happening with your father. I'm afraid that in his role as magistrate of Changsha your father has opened a hornet's nest. At this point, he—we—don't know who or what is behind this threat. Your father is fairly certain that it is related to one of his active cases, but he's not sure which one. He's working on several, including an instance of tax fraud, a series of thefts that seem to be related to each other, and an apparent murder. Each case is more involved than normal and has, therefore, taken a substantial amount of his time. In fact, he suspects that these diverse cases may actually be related and that a local power broker is involved. And it's even possible that fellow is himself simply a cog in the wheel of a wider criminal network involving political connections. At the same time, your father must also leave open the possibility that each crime is separate from the others. As you can see, the situation is quite complicated." Judge Hsu pulled at his beard and gazed intently at Mei-hua.

She began to feel uncomfortable and restlessly shifted her weight from one foot to the other. What was he thinking? Was he going to change his mind about telling her?

"Actually," Hsu asserted, "he's fairly certain, as am I, that there *is* a criminal network involved in this and that his investigations are a threat to its leader and their organization. No single criminal could put into play the flow of misinformation and outright lies designed to trigger a charge of treasonous behavior like the one we find being set up against your father. Further, we both suspect that this network may lead all the way to the Emperor's inner circle."

Mei-hua froze. From the beginning, when the Emperor's soldiers came to Changsha's court to talk to her father, she thought top government officials could be involved.

Although she had hoped she was wrong, it now looked as if her suspicions were confirmed.

Hsu held Mei-hua in his gaze. "Yes, I see you understand the significance of what I've just told you." He picked up his brush, slowly turning it between his fingers. "Unfortunately, there's more." He glanced away, then back.

Mei-hua kept her face as blank and calm as possible, even as her head was reeling.

He retrieved his brush and slipped it back and forth between his fingers. Finally, he said, "Your father has learned, through a secret source, that your whereabouts have definitely been discovered. While he doesn't know who unearthed this information or what resources they had, it appears that in all likelihood a spy has indeed been dispatched to monitor you and your activities."

Mei-hua flinched. The presence of a spy was something she and Judge Hsu had long suspected. They had been so careful. Outside of a handful of people, she wondered who else could possibly know her real identity and whereabouts.

"When I consider my new staff and who this spy could be, assuming he or she was not a part of my staff before, I have only one realistic prospect." He carefully and deliberately laid his brush down across a small dish. Straightening his shoulders, he said, "This is a person who has come highly recommended, who is involved in our everyday activities, and, therefore, has access to intimate information on every member of the household, including you."

Mei-hua stared at the floor. There could only be one person who fit Judge Hsu's description; someone they had earlier determined was a likely culprit. However, the subject hadn't been mentioned again in a long time. She had begun to believe Judge Hsu thought those past suppositions were not true.

She didn't want to hear what she knew was coming.

Hsu nodded, "You seem to have guessed who this person is: Soldier Guo."

Mei-hua felt the ground sway under her feet. A buzzing replaced the silence that had previously filled her head. Soldier Guo had saved her more than once; he had become a trusted and welcome part of her life. Now Hsu was telling her he really was the spy fighting against her and her father? How could that be? Was he so good at pretending when he really didn't care about her or her family except as targets, as enemies to his boss, whoever that may be?

Hsu watched her. He raised his hand again, this time in a wide, expansive gesture. "Choices, Mei-hua. Choices. We may not all have choices. We all started to trust this young soldier, it's true. But remember he is, first, an adopted son of the powerful eunuch Lord Chiu and, second, a soldier for his Imperial Majesty. His loyalty must lie with these two before all else. It is only then that he could act on other loyalties he may have. We, you, are far down on his list. He has no choice, you know that. Filial piety is paramount for everyone, even the Emperor. It defines justice." Hsu glanced at the Xie Zhi crouching at the entrance and exhaled loudly.

"As you have probably figured out, this is a problem for us all. After recovering from the injuries Soldier Guo incurred while protecting you in your last fray..."

Mei-hua touched her forehead at the memory of her close encounter with death when she was trying to help her friends, the carpenter and his wife. There was no doubt Soldier Guo saved her life. She struggled to listen to Judge Hsu.

"...he has been reassigned to my court through Lord Chiu. I cannot risk offending Lord Chiu—or the Emperor—by dismissing him and sending him back. Nor can I assign him minor duties and put him out of contact with my court activities. So, even if he is a spy—and there's every indication that he may be—we are stuck with having him close. In this continued role as a soldier for the court, he can easily keep an eye on you and your whereabouts.

"It's a dilemma." He absently swiped his fingers over his writing brush.

Mei-hua struggled to hold her tongue. If this were her father, she'd have no problem speaking. Judge Hsu was good to her and treated her well, but she didn't know how he would react to a young girl offering advice. Such behavior was beyond the norm and not something his daughter, Ping-an, would even consider doing.

While she vacillated, Hsu studied her and nodded. "Go ahead, Mei-hua. It is obvious you want to say something. This concerns you. What do you have to say?"

She leaned forward. "Master Hsu, Soldier Guo has not been here long; however, he has proven to be honorable and faithful in his duties to protect me and your court."

Hsu nodded.

"I humbly suggest that, since you can't dismiss him, we keep him even closer. That he not only remain in your service, since you have no options there, but also be reassigned as my personal guard."

Hsu raised his eyebrows in surprise.

Mei-hua hurriedly went on, "If he keeps that position, he won't suspect we believe he's an undercover agent. You implied he spied for Lord Chiu..." She looked up at Hsu for affirmation.

He nodded and waved for her to continue.

"If we keep him close, we'll control what he knows and can see. Plus, we will also be able to watch him to discover who he has contact with and how he passes on information."

Mei-hua spoke with conviction, but she hoped against all hope that they were wrong about Soldier Guo. She wanted him to be only what he at first appeared to be—her protector.

Judge Hsu pondered this for a moment, then said, "Not a bad idea. However, I hesitate to put you at risk. We don't know what he'd do if he were ordered to...shall we say, *dispatch with*...you."

Mei-hua bent her head, then looked up at his chin once more. "Perhaps Guei-lung could also come. His presence would certainly hamper anything Soldier Guo may try to do."

Hsu studied her through heavily lidded eyes for a few seconds before replying. "Such a plan may be the best thing to do given the circumstances. Guo will stay as your guard and Guei-lung will accompany you as well. This may work. However, if it doesn't, I will have failed your father and you, for the consequences could be fatal!"

Chapter 2

MEI-HUA MEANDERED BACK to the women's quarters where she shared a room with Ping-an. Lost in thought, she turned over the news from Judge Hsu. She simply didn't want to believe Soldier Guo was a spy working against her father. He had saved her life. It didn't make sense that he might also be a threat to her. But what other explanation could there be?

The heady fragrance of the courtyard's moist garden soil announced summer and new beginnings. A crisp, cool breeze coursed along the veranda and tugged at her silk skirt, causing it to flutter around her ankles. She pulled her knee-length cotton tunic closer. On its front panels, red bats flew through luminous white clouds. A special gift from Madam Wu, Ping-an's mother, the tunic provided more than warmth. Through its embroidered bats and clouds, the garment conveyed good fortune on the wearer.

Mei-hua fingered one of the downward flying bats. Although not usually one to believe in superstitions or emblems of luck, she hoped now that these symbols of prosperity truly would help her avert danger and protect the life of her father.

Several servants from local shops carrying scrolls and packages filed past her, heading toward Madam Wu's chambers. She watched them hurry along. Their blowsy, short work jackets billowed out behind them in the breeze, making the harried workers resemble fat toads as they rushed ahead of her. The impression lasted for only an instant as the line of servants disappeared through an open door.

Back in her own room, Mei-hua found one of Madam Wu's younger maids waiting. The girl brought a message: Ping-an was with her mother and they expected Mei-hua to come as soon as she returned from her meeting with Master Hsu. Mei-hua sighed. She needed to think about what she'd learned from Master Hsu, but she couldn't delay in attending to Madam Wu. Without pause, she turned around and headed back out onto the veranda.

Even before she reached her destination, she heard laughter spilling out into the courtyard. Inside Madam Wu's chamber, Ping-an and her mother stood over a cluster of objects laid out on the floor. Several unrolled scrolls; red window paper cut-outs trimmed in gold; multi-colored squares of painted pictures for doorways; long, thin, red scrolls with characters written down their length; and human-like figures made out of plants all lay in a jumble at their feet. The servants she'd seen earlier collected together along one of the walls.

"Mei-hua," Ping-an called, "come and see what we have. Today we must begin to prepare for Duanwu. You're in time to help us decide." Duanwu was the month of the Dragon Boat Festival—a time to chase out any potential evil lurking in the house, as well as prevent any other malevolent forces from attacking the home and its members. Good luck symbols and protective images were placed all about the compound on doorways, windows, and walls. Mei-hua glanced at Madam Wu. It was not up to Ping-an to decide if she should help; only Madam Wu could do that.

"Yes, come, Mei-hua. We need a large scroll to hang at the entrance to the residence, as well as auspicious scrolls and pictures of the demon chaser, Zhong Kuei, for each family member's room. Come. Help us decide."

Duanwu, the fifth lunar month, marked the summer solstice—the longest day of the year—and the true beginning of summer. This was one of Mei-hua's favorite celebrations and an especially exciting day in southern China. Along with its welcome warmth and nourishing rains, however, summer also brought insects and vermin. Thus, Duanwu celebrated new beginnings while also banishing evil. It was much like the earlier Shangsi Festival, although larger and more fun. The Duanwu Festival itself, which occurred on the fifth day of the fifth month, would be in five days and included dragon boat races, picnics, and romps in the countryside. However, because it was also a time to chase away malevolent spirits, people were mindful of the need for protection for the entire month.

After lengthy discussions over each item, they finally chose scrolls to be pasted on door jams. They also chose several pictures of Zhong Kuei crushing a demon with his foot, while proffering a bat that appeared ready to fly out of his open hand. Zhong Kuei would stand guard at each family member's door, while another impressive image on a long scroll would hang at the residence's entrance.

"Mei-hua, you must choose two scrolls with auspicious sayings and a picture of Zhong Kuei for Mr. and Mrs. Mu," Madam Wu said. "By giving them this Duanwu gift, you'll show them proper honor and respect." She picked up a brightly colored image of Zhong Kuei holding a bat high in his hand, a demon's cringing body scarcely seen under his massive foot. "It is only right, after all they've done for you. You owe them a life-long debt." And then, without waiting for her to choose, Madam Wu handed the scrolls and picture to Mei-hua.

The young woman took the bundle and bowed. Although Mei-hua recognized the affection behind her mistress's words, Madam Wu did not need to remind her of her special relationship with the Mus. After all, Mei-hua had saved Mr. Mu's life only a few weeks ago, and she herself was alive thanks largely to the protection and generosity once bestowed upon her by the humble couple. They were forever tied together.

"Thank you, Auntie," Mei-hua said.

Ping-an's mother frowned as she stared at Mei-hua, then said, "Master Hsu has given you the right to leave the house—with an escort, of course. Therefore, I will allow you to take these gifts to the Mus yourself today. As long as you have a guard to attend to you," she added sternly.

Mei-hua bowed again. Other than for visiting relatives, she knew Madam Wu normally did not approve of any of the family's women or their female servants leaving the compound. The fact that she was telling Mei-hua to go to the carpenter's home indicated that these instructions actually came from Judge Hsu, since the decision had to be against his wife's wishes.

"May I go along?" Ping-an piped up eagerly.

"No. Definitely not," Madam Wu said. "Your place is here."

Ping-an pouted, but said nothing. She rarely left the house and Mei-hua guessed she didn't really expect her mother to let her go to the simple quarters that made up the carpenter's home and shop.

"Mei-hua," Madam Wu said, "you'd best leave as soon as possible. That will give you time to visit without having to rush back before dark. I'll let Master Hsu know you'll be outside the compound and he'll arrange for your escort." She took up several long, thin papers with auspicious sayings. "Run along now. I have to tend to getting these scrolls and pictures hung in the proper places." With that, Madam Wu dismissed the girls, who gratefully left her oversight.

Back in their room, Ping-an said, "I wish I could go, too. I never leave the house except to visit family or friends." She sat on the raised platform in their room, resting her head in her hand and watching Mei-hua, who tied the scrolls and Zhong Kuei's image into a package and wrapped them in fine cotton.

Mei-hua nodded, although there wasn't much to say. She would have liked for Ping-an to come along as well. Mrs. Mu enjoyed her light banter and cheerful disposition. Having the two girls visit filled an empty space in her childless marriage.

Without warning, Orchid, Madam Wu's senior maid, burst through the door. "Ping-an!" she breathlessly exclaimed, clearly relieved to have caught the girls before Mei-hua left. "Your mother says you can join Mei-hua in visiting Mr. and Mrs. Mu. She wants you to take this to them as a Duanwu gift from the Hsu family." Having delivered her message, she regained her composure while holding out a package emitting an intense fragrance.

"Oh, how wonderful," Ping-an said, clapping her hands. With a happy giggle, she took the bundle and flipped its cloth enclosure aside. A small, doll-like figure of fastened mugwort stems lay against the creamy cloth. Mugwort was a special herb used to exorcise evil spirits and, when fashioned into a human-shaped talisman, its power to keep the household safe and healthy was amplified. During the Duanwu month, the talisman could be seen hung on doors across the city.

"Perfect," Mei-hua said with a grin. "Mrs. Mu will be so happy to see you, too."

"Now, if only Guei-lung could come along," Ping-an said. "We could all visit together."

"I'm sure he will come with us, as will Soldier Guo," Mei-hua said, remembering her earlier conversation with Master Hsu.

Ping-an didn't ask why or how Mei-hua knew this, and instead started prattling on about what to wear. She directed her maid to bring her a tunic of shimmering yellow silk embroidered with colorful butterflies. Slipping it on, it fell just below her knees, allowing the pale blue of her silk skirt to peek out along the bottom. Tiny embroidered butterflies also covered her lotus shoes.

Just as Mei-hua and Ping-an finished their preparations, a servant announced that the palanquins were ready to take them to the carpenter's house. With a maid on either side of Ping-an to assist her in the walk, they leisurely made their way to the household's outer courtyard.

Three palanquins sat in the courtyard's center, waiting for them. To protect the riders' privacy against strangers' eyes, the enclosed carriers each included curtains covering the windows and door. Four sinewy men waited at each sedan chair, ready to hoist their burden and proceed to the carpenter's home. Ping-an's brother would ride in one palanquin while Mei-hua and Ping-an would be together in another. Two of Ping-an's maids would ride in a third.

Ping-an giggled again when she saw her brother standing next to the carriers. "We're here! We're here and ready to go," she cheerfully called out to him.

Guei-lung smiled. "This will be a nice outing for you two. It's the first day of Duanwu and already the streets are starting to fill up with carts selling all kinds of things. Food, herbs, pictures, anything you could want. But," he added with a tone of command, "keep your curtains closed because there are also many strangers about."

His telling them how to behave irritated Mei-hua, but Ping-an seemed to accept his order. After all, as her older brother, she knew it was his right and duty to make sure she behaved properly. Mei-hua glanced over at another young man in uniform standing at the front of the palanquin grouping. Soldier Guo. As usual, without seeming to stare, he was watching them with a wry smile. He would guide the palanquins through the city streets.

The trip over to Mr. and Mrs. Mu's place was uneventful, although, as Guei-lung said, the streets were unusually crowded even for the always bustling city of Hangzhou. The market sounds of haggling and merchants calling out to passersby rang in their ears. Already the spicy fragrance of street food began to waft into the closed carriers before they even left the compound gates. The girls glanced at each other, grinned, and then bent toward their respective windows, making a small opening between the curtain and window frame.

"Look at those acrobats," Ping-an squealed. "That girl must not have any bones! She's bent in half!"

Mei-hua leaned over Ping-an to peer out on her side. A circle of people surrounded a trio of acrobats. A young girl had flipped over backwards and, with one leg projected straight out, balanced on top of a human tower created by an older man and a girl about their age. A large circle of people watched them intently. As the audience remained enthralled, an older woman moved amongst them, rattling a gourd to collect donations.

With her eyes locked on the scene, Mei-hua shivered. The entertainer made a living, but it wasn't easy and it wasn't much. Most of the time, they lived on the streets or in hovels. She closed her eyes, and thought: *If it weren't for the Mus and for Master Hsu and his family, I would also be living on the streets.* She gripped Ping-an's hand.

Ping-an, who remained enchanted by the acrobats, absently patted her arm.

At the carpenter's shop, the parade of palanquins stopped and they all disembarked. Mr. and Mrs. Mu, their faces beaming with wide smiles, came out onto the street to greet them.

"Mei-hua, Ping-an, it's so good to see you two. And, of course, you too, Guei-lung. Come in, come in." Mrs. Mu grabbed Mei-hua's arm and led them into the shop. Ping-an, leaning on her maids for stability, followed, with Guei-lung and Mr. Mu bringing up the rear.

The heady fragrance of camphor and other woods engulfed them as they entered the shop's darkened interior. In the familiar dimness, Mei-hua breathed deeply. *No perfume could be better than this*, she thought.

The Mus led them past mounds of boards ready to be made into furniture, chests, and coffins. Entering the back of the shop, the camphor aroma gave way to the scent of garlic and onion. This was their private area, which included their living and sleeping space as well as the kitchen. A thin shaft of light filtered through the lone window, barely brightening the room.

Soldier Guo remained at the entrance where he could keep an eye on them but not be intrusive.

"We can open the outside door to let in more light," Mrs. Mu said, shuffling over to the door and pushing it ajar. The sun streamed in, highlighting the simple, but clean, room. She'd barely started back to rejoin her guests when two little heads appeared at the opening. They remained in the doorway, staring at those gathered inside. Mrs. Mu shifted her attention to the new arrivals. She gestured to one of the children to come to her side. "Go to the cart on the corner and buy six meat-filled *baozi*," she said. "Pick out the largest dumplings you see." Mrs. Mu grinned as she gave the boy a couple of copper coins. Clutching the money in a tight fist, the child ran off down the alley.

"Do you know those children?" Mei-hua asked.

"No. They're not neighborhood children. With the festival just days away, there are a lot of people from the country who've come to see the dragon boat races. Their parents could be here to make a few extra coppers from the crowds, too."

"We did see lots of new carts and an acrobatic troupe on our way here," Mei-hua said. She caught Guei-lung glowering at her from where he stood behind Mrs. Mu. Clearly, he had realized she and his sister did not keep the curtains closed as he told them, and now he was miffed.

Mei-hua and Ping-an gave the gifts to the Mus and received a package in return. Neither opened their bundles but placed them to the side.

"Please sit and have tea with us," Mr. Mu invited them, gesturing toward the narrow *kang* built along one wall. The girls sat on the kang and Guei-lung joined Mr. Mu sitting cross-legged on a clean mat on the floor nearby. Mrs. Mu busied herself with heating water and preparing cups. When the child returned with the baozi, she served the steamed dumplings along with cups of a fragrant, freshly brewed beverage.

Mei-hua and her friends sat and talked with Mr. and Mrs. Mu for a long time. The tea complemented the pork in their dumplings. Mei-hua nibbled on the bun with a sip of tea in between, which cleansed her mouth after each bite. With the sun pouring into the room, adding a comfortable warmth, Mei-hua began to feel tired. She peered over at Ping-an and Guei-lung, who also showed signs of sleepiness.

"Honorable uncle and aunt," Mei-hua began, referring to them as such because, even though they were not really related to one another, they were now as close to her as family. "Thank you for your hospitality. Unfortunately, now we must return. Madam Wu will be expecting us and will want to hear how you both are doing."

"If you go to the dragon boat races, be sure and visit us again," Mr. Mu said.

"We will come if it is at all possible. My mother has planned many activities, however, so it may be difficult to get away," Guei-lung said.

Mei-hua and Ping-an nodded. They all knew how full the fifth day of the fifth month—the actual day of the Duanwu Festival and the dragon boat races—would be. Every year, Madam Wu, as with most people, filled the day with things that had to be done: gathering herbs, special baths, special foods. She insisted on each family member participating. This was the most important day of the year for dispelling evil and bad luck. No one could take the chance of ignoring it. Later in the day, there would be picnics or dinners to enjoy with family and friends.

After a long period of saying good-bye and wishing each other well, Mei-hua's little group languidly moved out of the house and onto the street. Their palanquin rested against the carpenter shop's wall. Soldier Guo went ahead and instructed the carriers to be ready.

Once Ping-an's maids had her securely settled in the second palanquin, Mei-hua stepped in and joined her. Just as they both managed to sit comfortably next to each other in such tight quarters, Guei-lung's head popped through the door's thick drapery.

"Now keep your curtains closed," he growled in a low voice. "How many times do I have to tell you two? It's not appropriate for young women to be peeking through the windows. What would Mother think?" With that, he stepped away and, seeing that the maids had already entered the last carrier, swung up and into the lead palanquin. As Mei-hua let the drapery fall into place, she caught a glimpse of Soldier Guo striding to the front and gesturing for the carriers to pick up the enclosed chairs.

Giggling, the two girls immediately each opened a peep hole in their curtains, allowing them to see what was going on as they passed through the crowds. This was not an opportunity to be missed. There were too many exciting things going on in the streets as people prepared for the dragon boat racing day and celebrated the Duanwu Festival.

Soldier Guo called out an order for the carriers, and the palanquins rocked up onto their shoulders. They started through the street at a slow pace. The intoxicating fragrance of herbs, spices, and luscious holiday buns, and other steamed or fried treats, competed with the humid smells of air heavy with impending rain and moist earth. The sharp stench of human waste momentarily filled the palanquin as a man passed by carrying two enormous, weighty buckets that severely bent the bamboo pole supported on his shoulders. Mei-hua opened her peep hole a bit more and stared at him. *I wonder how far he has to carry that load before he gets to the farmland it will fertilize*, she thought. *We could use it in our gardens*. Then she leaned back against the hard wall, smiling. *Our gardens*. How easily she had slipped into being a part of the Hsu household.

She put her arm through Ping-an's. This really was her family.

Without looking, Ping-an rested one hand on Mei-hua's arm; she maintained the peep hole in the curtain with the other. "Look, there—a street opera!" she said excitedly.

Mei-hua also returned to her opening. Strains of music played on the two-string, bowed *erhu* scraped against her ear. The instrument accompanied a woman singing a complaint in a high-pitched, whiny voice. Mei-hua strained to see the opera, but it was on the other side of the street, beyond her vision. As she pushed the hole open further, she could see more of the crowd milling around the musicians and singers, but the opera itself eluded her. Unexpectedly, a familiar figure stood out in the audience.

She blinked. It couldn't be. There, among the press of spectators was Ching Da, the head of the local secret society. Besides being wanted by the courts, he was also the only person she truly hated. She was convinced he was a part of the conspiracy to destroy her father. As she watched him, he turned and looked directly at their caravan. Dropping back inside, she let the curtain fall into place.

"What's the matter, Mei-hua? You look ill," Ping-an grabbed the arm Mei-hua had tucked through hers.

Not wanting to alarm her companion, Mei-hua shook her head. "The smells, they are too much."

"Yes, yes, of course." Ping-an dropped her curtain. "They are terribly strong—especially the night soil, don't you think?"

Mei-hua nodded, appreciating Ping-an's consideration. In spite of the fact that her friend rarely had an opportunity to be out, she was more worried about helping Mei-hua than enjoying the street scenes.

"You look pale. Rest your head against my shoulder," Ping-an suggested.

Mei-hua readily complied. On the one hand, she didn't want to worry Ping-an. But, on the other, she wished she could tell her friend about the sick feeling engulfing her as she remembered her last, awful confrontation with Ching Da. She laid her head on Ping-an's thin shoulder.

Suddenly, the palanquin lurched abruptly from side to side, throwing the two girls together. Mei-hua heard Ping-an's head thump hard against the back of the carrier. Her eyes shut and her head slumped forward onto her chest.

"Ping-an! Are you all right? Please, say something," Mei-hua called out, frightened by her friend's limp body. She sharply patted Ping-an's face to wake her up.

Ping-an moved her head and, barely opening her eyes, pushed Mei-hua's hand away. "I'm all right," she managed to say. "Stop hitting me."

Mei-hua laughed in relief as she gave her friend a big hug, but they were still in trouble. The palanquin again rocked wildly. She wrapped her arms protectively around Ping-an, afraid that her friend would hit her head again, perhaps with even more severe consequences.

What was happening? Was there a riot? Soldier Guo's razor-like voice cut through the air with orders, but she couldn't make out what he said. Guei-lung's screams—more orders, she assumed—intertwined with Soldier Guo's. The noise of the crowd never wavered.

"Stop him! Stop him!" Guo's voice broke through the din loud and clear.

Chapter 3

LOOKING OUT HER WINDOW, Mei-hua could see that the carriers had reached a narrow turn in the road where the crush of people had forced their sedan chair to fall behind and become separated from Guei-lung's. Whenever a small opening appeared between the palanquins, the crowd pushed through the space to create an even greater gap. The carriers struggled forward, but without Soldier Guo clearing the way, it was impossible for them to keep up or avoid the swarm of jostling shoppers and tourists.

"Grab onto the window jam to keep from being thrown about," Mei-hua called to her friend as she seized the window frame closest to her with both hands to steady herself.

With a small cry, Ping-an—eyes wide with terror—clung to the frame, clenching it so tightly her knuckles turned white. Then, closing her eyes, she pressed her forehead against her hands, stuck a foot out against the opposite wall, and fought to keep her body rigid so she wouldn't fall.

Mei-hua nodded, glad Ping-an wasn't screaming and listened to what Mei-hua said.

Still clutching the palanquin's window frame, Mei-hua caught hold of its heavy curtain's bottom edge. Without letting go, she cautiously slid one hand along the frame, scrunching the curtain as she did so. Finally, she had moved it enough to give her a good view of the street. Without concern for propriety or being seen, she stuck her head out of the careening window and looked at the two carriers on her side. They gripped their poles tightly. Short of being knocked over, they wouldn't drop their burden, but the press of people made it difficult for them to keep the palanquin steady.

Mei-hua turned her attention to the surrounding crowd. Several bedraggled men clustered near each of the carriers, jostling them. *Was it by accident or on purpose?* she wondered. Something made her look up and over the heads of the throng. There was Ching Da, again. Watching. He caught her eye and held it.

"Move away! Move back!" a sharp voice rang out and the crowd began to give the palanquins space once more. The scruffy knot of men harassing the carriers melted into the mass of people. Almost as soon as they disappeared, Soldier Guo came into sight. He brandished a cudgel, striking anyone who didn't move away from their palanquin fast enough. The cries of pain that erupted as the club landed on an unfortunate soul told everyone he meant business. A few yelled back at him, but once they caught sight of his soldier's uniform, they simply turned away with a grumble.

"Keep moving until you catch up with the lead sedan chair," Guo ordered the men. Then, for a brief moment, he caught Mei-hua's eye. He didn't say anything about her head hanging out of the window, although she thought he gave her a quick look of exasperation.

Their chair righted itself and began to move forward more smoothly. Mei-hua searched the crowd for Ching Da, but he had disappeared. With one hand still holding the curtain back, she turned toward Ping-an, who continued to clutch the window's frame to keep from being thrown against the palanquin's walls.

"You can let go, now," Mei-hua told her. "Soldier Guo cleared the crowd away and we've caught up with Guei-lung."

"Oh, that was so exciting," Ping-an said and smiled brightly as she settled into her seat once more.

Mei-hua looked at her in surprise. "Weren't you terrified?"

"Yes, yes, of course, but how exciting!" She rubbed her hands together and grinned again. "Besides, we're safe now. Soldier Guo saved us from being tipped over by those rude and unruly people."

"He did. He did, indeed," Mei-hua responded, even as she wondered if their near accident was indeed an accident caused by an unruly crowd. She didn't think those ruffians harassing her servants were there by chance; they were trying to make the chair tip over. With a quick glance at Ping-an, she decided not to disclose either her suspicions or the fact that she saw Ching Da lurking about. There was no reason to make her friend worry.

The two remained silent, each wrapped in her own thoughts, for the rest of the short trip back to the Hsu compound.

As soon as they arrived, Guei-lung jumped out of his carrier and dashed over to them. Their feet had barely touched the ground when he started talking in a low voice, clearly not wanting to be heard by anyone else.

"Come, let's go to the bamboo garden. We need to talk."

He cast a surreptitious glance in the direction of his mother's rooms. The girls nodded.

He looked at Guo, sighed, and strode ahead of the girls, leaving them to follow behind him. Mei-hua stepped unhurriedly along with Ping-an, who rested a hand on each of her maids' arms as they helped her walk along. After thrusting one of her lotus feet against the wall in the carriage to stabilize herself during their escapade, Ping-an was especially sore. Therefore, she had to walk to the garden even more slowly than her normal, leisurely pace.

Soldier Guo remained outside the private quarters. He was to report back to Judge Hsu.

"That was quite an exhilarating ride, wasn't it?" Mei-hua said to the maids. "Were you frightened?"

They both looked at her with blank expressions.

"The way our palanquins almost tipped over in the street," Mei-hua said, clarifying what she meant.

The maids shook their heads. "We didn't have any trouble," Lotus Blossom said. "There was that spot we slowed down and we heard Soldier Guo shouting orders, but we didn't know why. We thought there was some problem in the street and he had to clear it up." The other maid nodded her head in agreement.

Ping-an looked at them, eyes wide with curiosity. "Your carrier didn't almost tip over?"

"No, mistress," Lotus Blossom said. The two maids shook their heads in unison once more.

Mei-hua and Ping-an exchanged glances. That made the incident even more curious. Ping-an was about to ask them more questions when Mei-hua caught her eye and indicated with a slight shake of her head that she shouldn't say anything. Ping-an nodded her understanding and remained silent.

Mei-hua wanted to hurry into the garden and tell Guei-lung about the maids' experience, but Ping-an could only move so fast. By the time they arrived, Guei-lung had ordered tea and settled in near the bamboo garden's pond.

Before they reached him, he announced, "We need to discuss what to tell mother about that incident coming home."

"I agree," Ping-an said, a frown crossing her delicate features. "And when you hear what happened, or didn't happen, to my maids, you'll see we have an even bigger problem."

Mei-hua grimaced. She didn't like having their experience portrayed that way, even if it was true.

Guei-lung immediately demanded to be told about the incident. When they told him, he sharply sucked air through his teeth and squeezed his eyes shut as if shutting out the information.

"Oh, this is bad," he moaned. "Mother will not be happy."

"Whatever we tell her, Soldier Guo will have already given your father an accurate description and then surely he will tell Auntie about it all—and in detail," Mei-hua said, the corners of her mouth turning down.

"Oh, that's not good," Ping-an agreed, mirroring her brother and pouting. "She'll never let me out again. And maybe not you either, Mei-hua."

"Well, she doesn't have to learn that only our carriage was accosted. And maybe we can minimize the damage in her learning about what we can call 'the street incident,'" Mei-hua said.

"We really have to figure out how we can tell her something about 'the street incident' without her getting too angry and upset," Guei-lung said.

Mei-hua rolled her eyes; he just repeated what she'd said as if it was his original idea. But this was no time to argue; she let it go.

"It's Mother we're talking about," Ping-an said sardonically. "There's no way she's not going to be upset. And that means she'll be even more vigilant and watchful of what we—that is, Mei-hua and I—do, where we go, and when." She glanced meaningfully at Mei-hua. Then turned back to her brother, making a face at him she added, "You'll get to do whatever you like because you're a boy."

The bitterness in Ping-an's voice surprised Mei-hua. Ping-an always seemed to be the good, filial, and obedient daughter. Mei-hua had never really thought about how much her friend minded being housebound. After all, before coming to Hangzhou, when she lived in Changsha with her father, Mei-hua was also kept at home and seldom went out except for visits to family or friends.

"It's not my fault you're a girl," Guei-lung said. "It's your fate." Then, trying to lighten his sister's mood, he teased, "You should behave better and then you'll come back as a boy in your next life. Like me!" He threw his arms open in a grand gesture and grinned. Ping-an refused to be consoled. Her maids assisted her as she sat on a garden stool near her brother.

"Fate or no fate, karma or not, I don't see how the gods could think you're better than me, just because you're a boy and I'm a girl. You're always in trouble and I try to do everything I can to please Mother." Ping-an stuck out her lower lip and sighed.

Mei-hua flopped down, tucking her legs under her skirt. There was nothing to say. She agreed, it did seem unfair, but what could anyone do? He was right about one thing at least: it was their fate.

Guei-lung shrugged his shoulders. A breeze brought the heady fragrance of buns filled with lotus seed and red bean paste intermingled with the light aroma of green tea. As the sweet and spicy scents encircled him, he shifted his attention to an approaching attendant.

Mei-hua grinned: food always distracted him, even now, when they had just returned from a meal with the Mu's.

"Here. Place the dishes here," he ordered, pointing to a simple rectangular table to his right. The attendant placed a dish of buns, chopsticks, three translucent porcelain cups, and a pot of tea near the siblings. Ping-an reached over and started pouring tea, then she handed the cups around. Guei-lung picked up his chopsticks and grabbed a bun.

"What are you three doing in the garden?" Madam Wu's agitated voice shot through their gathering. As one, they turned toward her. "You should have come straight to my chambers and reported to me about your visit to Mr. Mu's."

Mei-hua flinched. Ping-an dropped her head. Guei-lung started to speak.

"No!" his mother said, pointing a finger at him. "I don't want to hear a bunch of excuses. I know what happened. Did you think I wouldn't find out? Accosted in the streets! And with a guard, who is obviously worthless." The words came out hot and furious.

"Mei-hua, how is it you can't stay out of trouble? Your escapade could have endangered not only yourself, but Ping-an and Guei-lung as well."

The unfairness of the diatribe chafed Mei-hua. She hadn't caused the turmoil, nor had the outing been her idea. Nevertheless, she did the only thing she could do: she tried to sooth her aunt.

"I'm so sorry, Auntie. It's true we had a difficult time because of the crowds. There is a lot of excitement on the streets with all of the people who are preparing for Duanwu and those who've come for the dragon boat races. But Soldier Guo managed to clear them away and here we are. Safe and sound," she said, keeping her eyes on Madam Wu's chin. She hoped no one would mention that only the girls' palanquin had been knocked about and the other two carriers were not manhandled to the point of almost tipping over.

"Well," Madam Wu said, "this will never do. I am responsible for you, for all of you, and this will *not* happen again." She pushed her hands into her jacket's long, wide sleeves and inhaled deeply before proceeding. "I'm not blaming you, Mei-hua, and I know it is important to you to visit with your old friends; however, it is not necessary for you, and certainly not Ping-an, to travel alone outside of the yamen. In the future, you can simply send gifts, messages, whatnot, through our servants. You will not be leaving the compound."

"But..." Mei-hua and Guei-lung began protesting at the same time.

Madam Wu's eyes flashed. "You all heard me. It's settled. No leaving the house!"

Chapter 4

MEI-HUA ENDURED A SLEEPLESS NIGHT. She lay listening to Ping-an's rhythmic breathing. Depressed, she turned on her side and watched a moonbeam travel across the room's floor as it transformed from a thin shaft of light just below the window to a long, pale streak leading across the room. *I wish that were my path*, she thought as she allowed her eyes to travel along the band of light ending at the door.

She switched to lying on her back. It was more and more difficult for her to accept her role as a protected young woman. *Meaning controlled*, she grumbled silently to herself. Sure, she had been protected in her father's home. She rested a hand over her forehead and eyes. But her father had also refused to have her feet bound, and allowed her to follow her mother's Uyghur tradition. Uyghur women let their feet grow naturally. They didn't bind them and have the tiny lotus feet as was typical of the Han people, his people. More importantly, he'd given her as excellent an education as any son would have gotten. Plus, she grinned into the darkness, he let her study martial arts under their faithful servant, Old Lin. Until she had had to leave her home, she'd never felt the restraints typical of so many girls and women in China.

She curled up on her side. So much of her life seemed to be in other people's hands. It was so unfair.

Sleepless, these thoughts rumbled in and out of her mind until the blackness of night eventually gave way to the light of day. Groggy, with eyes scratchy from lack of sleep, she rose. Although the sun's rays were already brightening the room, no one else in this part of the house was awake. Mei-hua quietly slipped out of the room and onto the veranda. She stepped into the courtyard's garden, breathed the fresh air deeply into her lungs, and stretched. Going through some of the marshal arts' stances Old Lin taught her, she wondered if she'd ever be free. How could she help her father when she was a prisoner herself?

After a while, she returned to the room she shared with Ping-an and found her friend beginning to stir. Lotus Blossom had laid out her clothing. Without a word, Mei-hua sat near the window and stared out, waiting for the day to begin.

Later, while the two girls ate breakfast, a message came from Master Hsu. He wanted to see Mei-hua as soon as possible, before court began.

Once more she found herself standing outside his office, waiting for permission to enter. Finally, a guard led her inside. As she stepped past the powerful Xie Zhi to the middle of the room, she wanted to reach out and touch its flanks for good luck and to wish for justice. Justice for her family. Instead, she merely gave it a wistful, sidelong glance. Then, facing the judge sitting at his desk, she gave a low bow.

Without a word, he observed his charge for a moment.

"Step forward."

She approached.

"It seems you had quite an adventure yesterday."

Mei-hua felt her face grow hot and hoped he didn't notice her blushing. Dropping her gaze, she firmly clasped her hands together. As her sleeves fell down, covering her hands, she was relieved. The judge wouldn't be able to see how tightly her fingers were intertwined.

"Soldier Guo told me about the palanquin incident. He'd also noted that the maids' palanquin had not been bothered by the crowd and strongly felt you were being targeted by thugs. Though for what purpose, he couldn't say." He studied her intently, watching for a response.

Mei-hua tried to appear attentive, but remained silent. So, she thought balefully, Judge Hsu knew about their carrier being the only one in trouble. That wasn't good. On the other hand, she guessed that he hadn't told his wife. That was good. She glanced aside at this thought. If Madam Wu knew, as angry as she had been, her fury would have been even greater at the thought of her daughter and Mei-hua narrowly missing another run-in with criminals.

"Now, I want you to give me your perspective on what happened," he said. While he didn't sound angry or accusatory, he didn't sound especially sympathetic, either.

Mei-hua cleared her throat and barged ahead. "Uncle, everything Soldier Guo said is true. I don't know if it's related or not, but I did see the secret society leader, Ching Da, shortly after we left the Mu home and again during the incident. He appeared to be watching us." She cleared her throat again and shuffled back and forth on her feet. "He looked right at me while our palanquin was being tossed about. I'm sure he knew I was in it."

Judge Hsu thoughtfully touched his beard while he appeared to stare unfocused into the middle distance. Finally, he murmured, "Ah, Ching Da. Yes, he's back. My men have heard that he's tied in with the tea-horse trade merchants."

Mei-hua shifted her weight; she didn't have any idea what he was talking about. "I'm sorry, Uncle. I don't..."

"You don't know what the tea-horse trade system is? No reason you should, it's fairly new." He tapped his chin. "Our Honorable Emperor's cavalry is powerful, but its strength rests on having excellent war horses. Without an invincible cavalry, it would be close to impossible to keep the northern and other western barbarians at bay. However, we are always in need of sturdy and reliable steeds. Unfortunately, even with our excellent farms, we can't raise enough horses to keep our cavalry strong. The tribal peoples in the west have the best stock—the strongest and most steadfast—because they have raised and relied on horses for their livelihood for centuries.

"A few years ago, our Honorable Emperor started trading for their superior horses. We've been able to get thousands of the very best for the military in this way." He rested his elbows on the desk and intertwined his fingers.

"To control graft and price gouging, only merchants who've been given an official license from the Emperor can participate in this trading network. Our southern tea is in the greatest demand by these tribal groups. Therefore, our top grade tea is traded for their best horses, while middle-grade tea brings good horses for everyday cavalry use. However, as you might expect, lots of other goods are also traded, such as fine brocades, cotton cloth, spices, and sometimes even silver or gold."

Mei-hua nodded, but she still didn't see what any of this had to do with her and her father.

"So, as I said, getting the horses we need for a strong cavalry requires a large trading network. The merchants who get licenses can become extremely wealthy." He paused before continuing. "However, some people never have enough. We suspect that some legitimate merchants are also involved with a criminal secret society. Together, they are diverting goods, such as the high grade tea, and selling them on the black market.

Mei-hua listened carefully, waiting for any sign of a connection with her family and their problems. Thieves in Hangzhou and way off in the western part of the country—all of this was seemed too removed from her father's district.

"What's important to us," he continued, "is that the tea trade starts here in Hangzhou and moves west, through Changsha, your father's district, and then on to the tribal areas."

She perked up.

"Besides traveling through his district, it looks like the gang and its leader, whose identity we still haven't quite been able to discover, may very well be someone located in Changsha, not in Hangzhou."

Now it made sense. If the leader of the thieves was in Changsha where her father was magistrate, her father was probably pursuing him. In fact, she was sure he would be.

Judge Hsu watched her and nodded. "I see you understand the connection now. Yes, your father, as magistrate, is responsible for overseeing this whole tea-horse trade is secure as the trade goods pass through his district and that all the money and goods go where they should. Through confidential correspondence between your father and me, I know he has been investigating this matter. He believes the gang leader may be in Changsha. He also suspects that the gang is tied to a well-placed person. Perhaps a local elite or even someone with influence and power in the new dynasty. It would take someone with connections to be able to control the flow of such goods. To be able to siphon them off and into the black market." He nodded in confirmation with his own words. "Your father had a couple of good leads, but they've gone cold."

Mei-hua shivered. What could she do? She wanted to go home to Changsha and help. But would Master Hsu let her return? Would her father let her come home? No. She was sure neither would allow it. Perhaps she could do something from here, in spite of Madam Wu's diligence.

"We've discussed my investigating from this side to see what we can learn." He gently pulled on his beard in silence for a moment and then said, "Your seeing Ching Da here must mean the gang is planning something in Hangzhou. The officially sanctioned tea, along with other trade goods, will be sent out west as soon as the Duanwu festival is over. We are certain the criminals will act then. I've posted men to watch the Imperial warehouses. Hopefully, that will be enough."

Mei-hua tried to listen while a series of competing ideas clamored for her attention. If Ching Da was part of the gang trying to destroy her father, she would destroy him and his gang first. She would discover their identities and where they were. She would bring them to justice and prove her father's innocence to the world.

"Well, Mei-hua, I wanted to let you know what was happening. Being motherless, I realize you and your father are extremely close and you share a special relationship with him. For good or ill, he doesn't see you as a simple girl, but as someone who can be trusted with information. He wanted me to let you know these things. Nevertheless, you are here with my family and safe, so I'm confident this information won't cause you any trouble."

Mei-hua bowed in acquiescence. "Yes, Uncle."

"You may return to your room now," Judge Hsu said with a kindly expression. Having dismissed her, he took up his brush and began to sweep it across the ink stone on his desk.

"Uncle?"

He looked up, pausing his brush over the ink puddle. "Yes, speak."

"Because of the slight problem we had on the way back from the Mu family," she said, trying to minimize the carriage incident, "Auntie has forbidden Ping-an and me to go outside the compound. However, I need to run several errands. I am sure I will be safe with Guei-lung and Soldier Guo—now that we know what to watch out for."

He looked doubtful. So she quickly added, "Perhaps one more soldier could be assigned to come along. He could walk behind the carriage while Soldier Guo was in the front. That would certainly protect the palanquins."

"You are too independent for a girl," Judge Hsu commented dryly, putting his brush down.

Mei-hua sighed. She was stuck in the women's quarters.

"But," he went on, "I believe your father would be in agreement with my giving you more leeway in leaving the compound—as long as Guei-lung and two guards are always in attendance." He pressed his lips together momentarily, then said: "All right. You may go. I'll inform Madam Wu of my decision."

Mei-hua kept a smile off her face, but her heart soared. He had opened the door to her cage. She was now a falcon on the hunt. "Thank you, Uncle. I'll tell Ping-an."

He bent forward, "No. Not Ping-an. She must remain at home. Even I wouldn't dare change my wife's decision about her daughter." His eyes twinkled as he nodded. "Mothers are tigers when it comes to protecting their children. Which makes me think: you'll also need a maid to attend to you when you're out. It's not appropriate for a young woman such as yourself to travel around alone or only in the company of men. A maid should ameliorate some of Madam Wu's anxiety for you in this."

Mei-hua thanked him again and left, relieved that she would be free to move about. Somewhat free, she amended.

She immediately began formulating a plan. Yes, she was *only a girl*, she thought ruefully, but she would help her father. Beginning with Ching Da. She'd seen him in front of the store called the Golden Pheasant. Tomorrow, she'd go shopping.

Chapter 5

AS EXPECTED, MADAM WU WAS NOT HAPPY that her husband had given Mei-hua permission to leave the women's quarters again, even though Guei-lung, Soldier Guo, and another guard would always be with her.

"How can I trust that they will really be with you at all times? You have a terrible habit of disrupting even the best attempts to ensure your safety," she fumed.

"Please don't worry, Auntie," Mei-hua soothed. "I promise, nothing will happen. We will only go to a nearby shop. It's quite near."

Madam Wu puffed her cheeks in frustration; however, in spite of her strong objections, she assigned Lotus Blossom as Mei-hua's attending maid. It wasn't as good as keeping her adopted niece at home but, under the circumstances, it was the best she could do.

"And don't let her out of your sight. If she gets into any trouble, I will hold you accountable. Do you understand?" Madam Wu peered at Lotus Blossom.

The maid bobbed up and down several times as her mistress listed her responsibilities toward the unmanageable Mei-hua.

As Madam Wu went on, Mei-hua looked over at the maid. She was pleased. In spite of her club foot, Lotus Blossom had the strong, sturdy body of the country girl she was. And, in Mei-hua's opinion, she had a more adventurous spirit than the other maids. She wouldn't be easily overwhelmed at going out into the crowds and shops.

In the short time Mei-hua had lived with the Hsu family, she'd learned that Lotus Blossom came from a farming family and knew the bite of poverty too well. During a famine, her parents could no longer feed both of their children. Their best option was to sell one of them, and between their only son or only daughter, they had to choose their daughter. A son was not only responsible for caring for his parents in their old age, but his presence also ensured the continuation of the family line and the necessary performance of the ancestor worship rituals. Without these rituals, Lotus Blossom's parents would become hungry ghosts. Having no descendants to care for and honor them after their death, her parents' spirits would travel over the earth, causing harm because they were angry and unfulfilled. This meant that, devastated as they were to lose her, her parents' only choice was to sell their daughter to Madam Wu.

Selling Lotus Blossom into the Hsu household was a lucky choice for their daughter. With her club foot and plain face, all agreed it would be difficult to find her a good husband. As a maid, however, she had food, shelter, and a relatively easy life, especially compared to her parent's existence on their hard-scrabble plot. She would never suffer starvation again.

In return, Lotus Blossom showed her appreciation through an extreme loyalty and devotion to the Hsu family, and especially to Ping-an, her young mistress. When Madam Wu assigned her to Mei-hua in her external forays, Mei-hua hoped Lotus Blossom would extend her devotion to her as a part of the Hsu family.

As soon as the shops opened, Mei-hua ordered the palanquins to be readied. Guei-lung met her, grumbling and pulling at his grey robe, "I don't know why you have to go out so early. I've hardly finished eating."

"You don't look like you're starving," she teased.

"Not that you would care."

She pretended not to hear his last remark. "Lotus Blossom will be coming with us today," she said instead.

"Yes. Mother told me." He gave his robe a final tug. Squaring his shoulders, he looked down at her—he was proud of the fact that he was taller than Mei-hua. "You know she's quite upset. I hope nothing happens today." He cast a glance in the direction of his mother's rooms.

"We'll be fine." Mei-hua glibly responded. Master Hsu said she could go out and now she would. Madam Wu and a worrying Guei-lung were not going to stop her. "I see Soldier Guo is here and there's the second guard," she said, spying their escort.

The soldiers stood holding the reigns of two horses. Guo's uniform accented his broad shoulders; his hat shadowed his eyes so she couldn't tell where he was looking. Even so, she was sure she knew and turned her head away.

She glanced at the two palanquins in the courtyard. "Aren't you coming? I thought Master Hsu wanted you to accompany me." She cast an anxious look at Guei-lung. If he didn't come along, she might have trouble leaving the compound.

"I'm going, don't worry." He puffed out his chest. "But I'm not riding in the carrier; Soldier Guo and I will ride horses. That way, if anyone tries to hurt you, I can immediately respond. Those sedan chairs are too confining in an emergency."

Mei-hua nodded, satisfied that he would accompany her. Plus, she completely agreed about the horses. Yesterday's incident wouldn't have gotten so out of hand if Soldier Guo had been on horseback. Horses created another level of security against criminals who more than likely would be on foot.

"Where do you want to go? Mother said you want to shop for more Duanwu gifts?" He gave her a quizzical look.

"There was a shop called the Golden Pheasant not far from here. We passed it yesterday after leaving Mr. and Mrs. Mu's home."

"I know the one. I'll instruct Soldier Guo."

Mei-hua hid a grin. Guei-lung thrived on appearing to be in charge and able to give orders.

Lotus Blossom helped her into the front palanquin. The carriage tipped slightly as she stepped inside but evened out once she sat in its center. Then the maid climbed into the second enclosed chair.

The little procession filed out of the compound: Soldier Guo rode in front to clear the way, followed by Guei-lung, then Mei-hua and Lotus Blossom, and finally the second guard on foot. Mei-hua heaved a sigh of relief. The threat of Madam Wu sending a servant out to prevent them from leaving nagged at her until they cleared the yamen gates.

With a smile tugging at her lips, Mei-hua pushed the window curtain back and peered out into the active city life around them. As before, there were already quite a few people about. Most of the shops had opened and vendors were out with their carts, clogging the thoroughfare and slowing anyone not on foot or horse.

She delighted at being able to glimpse the scene unfolding around her. Women shopped for vegetables and meats; old men carried cricket cages to the park; and children ran through the streets laughing. A small puppet theater had been set up near the temple. And she recognized the acrobatic family she had seen yesterday. They enjoyed another enthusiastic audience this morning.

In no time, the litter halted and Guei-lung came to open her door. Before Mei-hua could even begin to step out, Lotus Blossom appeared to assist her.

"Are you sure this is where you want to shop?" Guei-lung asked, looking dubiously at the rather shabby storefront. Of all the businesses on the street, this one set the standard for the least maintained shop. While a freshly painted sign read Golden Pheasant and hung above the door, everything else about the place reflected neglect.

Mei-hua smiled at him. "Yes. Perfect."

He scowled. "You have odd taste."

She grinned again. "I'll explain later. There's a reason we're here." She had wanted to tell him about seeing Ching Da come out of this store, but she'd not had a chance and now she was afraid she'd be overheard. There was no time to tell him; he'd have to trust her.

Guo turned the horses over to the second guard and joined them. He remained at a reasonable distance, yet close enough to act if there were any sudden attack. From his position, she could now see his eyes. They alternately fixed on her and then swept around the area. He kept alert for any unusual happening. As she surreptitiously—she hoped—watched him, she again wondered how he could possibly be involved with those who wished to harm her and her father. Her heart begged the questions: How could this care, this protection, be a sham? Was it a mere device to get her to trust him and then...what?

His eyes swept back and locked with hers. *Insolent*, she thought as warmth flooded her face. Before she could turn away, his eyes swept past her and around the area. Embarrassed at her own reaction to his gaze, she looked down. She wondered if she'd imagined his stare. Perhaps he was simply looking past her into the shop. Focus, she reminded herself. Remember why you're here.

With Guei-lung striding along at her side and slightly in front, they entered the store. The only light came from the front door and window. Nevertheless, in spite of the dimly lit interior, it was immediately apparent that the merchandize was sparse and of mediocre quality.

A thin, bent man, wearing a somewhat shabby robe, stepped out of a back room and greeted them with an ingratiating smile. Guei-lung returned the greeting and engaged him in a conversation about the upcoming dragon boat races. It was the hottest topic of the day and one everyone enjoyed. The two discussed the various teams, and who they thought would win the races this year.

Looking around the room, Mei-hua noticed that Guo had disappeared and assumed he was outside with the horses and palanquins. She walked about with Lotus Blossom. The shop's wares were in disarray, scattered over the counter top and in several barrels running along either side of the back door. An impressive amount of dust lay over most of the goods. Mei-hua sneezed as she cautiously made her way to the rear of the shop, inspecting the merchandize as she moved along. Lotus Blossom followed, holding a sleeve over her mouth and nose to avoid breathing the dust-laden air. Now and then, with her brows drawn together, she looked over at Mei-hua.

Low voices tumbled out of the back room as they approached. Mei-hua couldn't understand what was being said, but it sounded like two men. She glanced at the merchant. He and Guei-lung remained engrossed in their discussion of the dragon boat races, comparing the merits of its teams. She casually took Lotus Blossom's arm and gradually ambled closer to the lowered voices, continuing to inspect the moribund merchandise as she did so.

Lotus Blossom began to look more and more distressed. Finally, she softly whispered in Mei-hua's ear, "Mistress, this is not a good shop. Really, everything here is inferior and too old. If you want to shop for Duanwu, I know of another excellent store."

Mei-hua read concern in her face. She patted Lotus Blossom's arm and quietly reassured her, "Don't worry. Right now this one will do."

Lotus Blossom shook her head and remained silent.

As they approached the barely ajar door, the voices became more distinct. After another quick glance back at the merchant, Mei-hua stepped over and peeked inside. Soldier Guo and Ching Da had their heads close together as they talked in the far corner of a room filled with shadowed forms.

Mei-hua's hand shot up to cover her mouth. She couldn't believe it. Suspicion was one thing, yet here was proof of Guo's betrayal. She felt a surge of anger. How dare he? Did he think he could manipulate her into thinking he could be trusted, making it easier for him to spy on them? She pressed her lips tightly together. Well, more than one could play this game. She'd not read *The Romance of the Three Kingdoms* and *The Art of War* for nothing, having learned about the importance of strategy in winning a battle. And now she had the advantage of knowing her enemy.

She abruptly pulled Lotus Blossom away as she walked to a table set up near the shop's front, just inside the entrance. Mounds of piles of fresh mugwort and calamus herbs called to her. As she passed the merchant on her way toward the front, she said, "A good friend told me your shop had a fine selection of mugwort and calamus—and at a reasonable price."

He smiled coyly, nodded briefly to Guei-lung, and followed her. The sweet, intoxicating fragrance of the herbs attested to their freshness.

"Yes, we got these in early this morning. They are the best you'll find anywhere." His voice was as sticky as honey and twice as sweet.

Mei-hua hid her disgust. Instead, she studied the fragrant herbs, examining several bunches. Even though several inches shorter than the merchant, Lotus Blossom stood watchfully between her and the obsequious man, never letting him get too close. He merely talked over the top of her head, telling Mei-hua all about his wonderful merchandize. Finally, she picked out one small bundle each of mugwort and calamus. Next to the herbs there were four sets of special

Duanwu sandals woven from calamus leaves. As with all mugwort and calamus herbs, they protected the wearer from evil. She picked up a pair.

"Ah, you'll not find a better pair anywhere in Hangzhou. I can give you a good price on them."

After bartering for a short time, Mei-hua left the shop with the herbs and the calamus sandals. However, their enticing aroma couldn't cleanse the bitterness that filled her heart from the moment she spotted Guo with Ching Da.

Chapter 6

CLOUDS OF DUST FROM PASSING CARTS rose to meet them as they stepped out into the street. Mei-hua coughed, caught her breadth, then coughed again. Her mouth tasted like dirt. She licked her lips, making it worse. Lotus Blossom appeared at her side with a large, green, silk handkerchief.

"Hold this over your nose and mouth. It will help," the maid said, handing it to her.

With the handkerchief covering the lower part of her face, Mei-hua stopped to take a couple of breathes through it. She stood amidst the clamor of street vendors and, as she paused, examined the buildings around them.

An almost equally shabby shop, the Western Branch, stood next to the Golden Pheasant; its entrance another dark hole.

"Let's go in there," she whispered to Guei-lung. "I saw Ching Da in the back room just now. Perhaps we can find out more about the owner of the Golden Pheasant and his business." She noticed Guo had surreptitiously rejoined them. His presence prevented her mentioning seeing him with Ching Da; he'd overhear. She'd tell Guei-lung later.

"It looks pretty much like the other one," Guei-lung grimaced. "How can they do any business? These are the most ramshackle shops I've seen in the city. What a waste of valuable space." Shaking his head in disapproval, he asked, "Are you sure you want to shop in this one?"

Mei-hua laughed and in a loud voice said, "In such a shop, we should be able to get the best prices." She didn't want Soldier Guo to guess her real reason for visiting the Western Branch.

Guei-lung muttered something under his breath, but led the way into the store. Mei-hua followed, accompanied by Lotus Blossom; Guo came up behind.

As they entered the dimly lit store, a tall, swarthy man with enormous, dark eyes hurriedly came from behind the counter, calling out a greeting to Guei-lung. A musky, dry odor, similar to that at the Golden Pheasant's, engulfed them. Shelves with small jars encrusted with grime ran along the walls behind the counters. Nevertheless, once inside, this shop didn't appear quite as dilapidated as its neighbor.

Large bags of rice, piled near the entrance, looked fresh, as if recently brought in. The floor around them was relatively dust free, due to many feet walking near the bags. At least this seemed to bring some money into the business.

Mei-hua meandered along the shelves with Lotus Blossom in tow. A shaft of light from the doorway fell over the rough countertop, spotlighting clumps of merchandize. Apparently, as with all the other shops in town, in order to take advantage of the Duanwu festival, the shop sold the familiar holiday talismans, figurines, and hairpins made of mugwort and calamus herbs.

Guei-lung went through the customary greetings with the owner, who ignored the young women. Guei-lung's more educated accent contrasted with the owner's forceful, even quarrelsome-sounding, tone. The interplay of their words crashed through the room.

A barrel-chested man entered and began picking through the stacks of Duanwu specialty items. From his clothing, Mei-hua thought he was a day laborer. His short coat hung off one shoulder, barely covering his torso; a rope at his waist kept his coat from completely falling into disarray. Another rope bound his leggings tightly at the knee. He muttered to himself as he picked up, looked at, and dropped one herbal figure after the other, paying no attention to where it landed, carelessly mixing the piles of mugwort and calamus. The owner hurried over to his side.

"I want one mugwort and one calamus. How much are they?" the customer demanded abruptly.

The owner gave him a price and the man began bargaining, which was not unusual. However, the customer's voice was loud and, Mei-hua thought, argumentative. As she watched, he angrily raised two figures and roughly shook them. Bits of herbs flew as the talismans started to unravel. The owner raised a soothing hand, but the customer shook the figures harder and tossed them onto the counter. Mei-hua could see they no longer held their human shape. One had an arm that was now an open, loose cluster of stems. The other lay in a bedraggled mass of stems and leaves. The customer grabbed for another figure, but—as his fingers began to wrap around it—the merchant quickly put his hand over it and pulled the figure away.

Mei-hua shot a glance at Guei-lung. He stood watching, not moving.

"Perhaps you would like to…" the shop owner started, but the customer interrupted with, "You are charging too much. You are nothing but a robber. All you foreigners come in here and want to rob us!" the customer yelled. "This is a new dynasty, a Han dynasty. Go back west where you came from." Spittle erupted from his mouth, flying in the merchant's face. The merchant recoiled and raised his hand to wipe his cheek. The customer laughed.

A movement caught her eye and she saw Guo stride quickly to the front. He came between the men. He stood a head taller than the customer, but was somewhat shorter than the merchant.

"It's time for you to go," Guo said to the belligerent customer. His voice was calm and authoritative.

The man looked at Guo and at his soldier's uniform. He tightened his lips into a frown and shook his head, locking his eyes with Guo's. "Why are you siding with this foreigner? They're all the same and we should banish every single one. Free our country once and for all from them. They're robbers, every one." Then, he spun around and stomped out of the shop.

The embarrassed merchant thanked Guo profusely.

"Never mind. The man was a bully and bullies are cowards. He was no threat to me." He gazed at the ruined figures hanging off the counter top. "Although I can't say the same for your merchandize."

"As you say, never mind. The gods take their own retribution. It is not up to me," the merchant said. Then he busied himself in straightening out his goods. Once satisfied with the appearance of the reconstructed piles, he returned to where he'd left Guei-lung. Without commenting on the previous scene, Guei-lung seamlessly continued their discussion of the Dragon Races.

Guo stepped back against a wall, the ever-quiet observer.

Mei-hua moved to the counter and surveyed the holiday items.

The clean fragrances of mugwort and calamus competed with the stale, dusty interior. Mei-hua recognized human-shaped figures similar to those Madam Wu distributed yesterday. The neat bundles of mugwort and calamus herbs were known as "the mugwort tiger and the calamus dragon," and were often hung together in doorways. Clustered as one, their power to protect against the evils of disease and disasters was amplified. She gently touched the magical figures, taking her time, while Guei-lung continued to befriend the owner.

An array of hairpins lay in shallow boxes near the mounds of human-like figures. Mei-hua began picking up each one and examining it. She marveled at their beauty. An artist had braided mugwort into delicately detailed tigers and attached the tiny animals to the end of long hairpins.

"These are the most superbly designed tigers you will find anywhere," an accented voice said.

She turned to find the owner towering over her. Instinctively, she stepped away from him and bumped into the counter. Where was Guo? She glanced quickly around the interior. He wasn't there. The room was too small for him to be lurking behind something or around a corner. He was gone. Again.

"Indeed, they are lovely," she said looking up into the penetrating, sunken eyes. Although he was clothed in the same long robe worn by most Chinese shop owners, she knew the aggressive customer had been right about the merchant not being Han. He was too tall, his eyes too round, and his non-local accent strong. She bit the inside of her cheek in thought. She felt she should recognize his accent, but couldn't quite place it.

"The detail is remarkable," Guei-lung interjected as he moved next to Mei-hua.

Grateful for his presence, she turned back toward the counter and picked up a hairpin to examine it. She asked the owner a few questions about the piece and the artist. He enthusiastically chatted about his wares.

Mei-hua held a long hairpin up against the back of Lotus Blossom's head, as if deciding how it would look. "Sir, you have an accent that I find familiar but can't place. Are you from Hangzhou?" she said in a conversational tone.

"Although I have been fortunate to have a shop here in Hangzhou for many years, I was born in an area sometimes called Xiyu in western China, a long, long way from here. Many people know it as being famous for its scholars and for its trade. A strange mix perhaps, but each tells a story of the region: one speaks to our brilliant and successful intellectuals, while the other reflects the economic success we have reached by raising the finest horses in the world." He smiled. "You may think I am bragging, but no. This is a matter of reality and I am proud to be a son of Xiyu."

"As you should be. Our home areas are a part of us," she said.

He seemed to be closely examining her face, her eyes, and then he passed a quick glance at her feet peeking out of her long, loose pants. "As you say," he bobbed his head in agreement. "My family is Uyghur," he added and left a silence open between them.

Although it seemed too personal to discuss with a stranger, Mei-hua nevertheless said, "My mother was Uyghur; my father is Han."

He nodded. "Welcome to my shop, little cousin," he said and smiled. "Now, are you interested in these hairpins? I can give you a special price on them."

Mei-hua turned back toward the counter and went through the cache of hairpins, discussing each one with the owner. Finally, she picked out two, one for Madam Wu and one for Ping-an.

"Do you know the owner of the Golden Pheasant?" Mei-hua asked casually as he wrapped the hairpins for her.

"Not well. He's been here as long as I have."

"He doesn't seem to have many customers," Mei-hua said, hoping to draw him out.

"This is not an auspicious area for a store. It used to be, but not anymore. Nevertheless, he never appears worried or concerned. Somehow he always has enough money to keep his business, to eat well, and to have a concubine." He smiled wryly.

"I hope to change my luck this year." He swept his hand around the room. A large mugwort figure hung on the door, and Mei-hua remembered seeing a similar one made of calamus on the outside. Also, a large image of Zong Kuei peered down into the room and a fine, brightly painted figure of another immortal had been placed on a small altar sitting against the back wall. Candles, small dishes of food, and a cup spread out around him. Although Mei-hua guessed the owner was probably Muslim, he was hedging his bets by trusting these familiar Chinese talismans and immortals to dispel the evil that had to be keeping good business away from his door.

"Do you know if he has any regular customers? People you would recognize?" Guei-lung asked.

Before the merchant could respond, a crash of pottery hitting the floor jerked them all to attention.

"Please forgive my clumsiness," Guo called out as he bent to retrieve unbroken pots from among a pile of broken bits and other debris. He had managed to bring down one of the shelves filled to overflowing with small clay vessels.

"Oh, my herbs!" the owner cried, rushing forward. "Stop! Let me! Let me! Don't touch anything, you will mix the herbs even more."

Guo backed away and stepped over to Mei-hua and Guei-lung. Sweet, vinegarish, spicy, and bitter fragrances seeped into the room. The potpourri of herbs wiped away the taste of dust that had formerly permeated the space.

"How could you be so clumsy?" Guei-lung lashed out. "Now we'll have to pay for all your damages!"

Guo bowed and clasped his hands before him. "I beg you to forgive such bad luck. I thought I had seen a ruffian outside and knocked the shelf loose when I turned to pursue him."

"Well," Guei-lung continued looking toward the street, "where is he now? I don't see anyone."

"As you say, he disappeared. The unfortunate accident delayed me too long."

Guei-lung sputtered, but appeared to be mollified.

Mei-hua watched Guo through narrowed eyes. Where had he gone while they were in the store? Did he knock the shelf down on purpose? But, if so, why? She peered through the open door. She hadn't noticed any strange activity outside. Besides, their guard was still within sight of the doorway. What was Guo up to now?

Chapter 7

THE TRIP BACK TO THE HSU COMPOUND was uneventful. A thin beam of light coming though Mei-hua's peephole almost brightened her litter's gloom. Raucous cries of street vendors blended with the throaty river of sounds coming from the market as buyers and sellers argued over prices and shared gossip. Multiple languages clashed against each other, and Mei-hua wondered how people in this dynamic city managed to communicate at all.

An imposing and daunting entrance, with a fine gold lettered placard over it, announced their arrival at the yamen's gate. Neighing and stomping, Guo's horse waited impatiently for the massive doors to open and allow the entourage to enter. Although short, the tawny steed had a fiery nature and demanded respect. Mei-hua strained to catch a glimpse of it as Guo rode it into the yamen's public courtyard.

Their little procession passed through the public area of the compound and into the family's private courtyard. As soon as the litter stopped, Mei-hua jumped out. She stood near it, talking with Guei-lung, by the time Lotus Blossom reached her side. The maid's disapproval was palpable. Her mistress was supposed to wait and be helped out of the litter. It was Lotus Blossom's duty to assist. Besides, young ladies did not jump around; they descended with grace and refinement. She quickly surveyed the courtyard to see if anyone from the women's quarters had seen them come in.

Mei-hua noticed her checking for observers. "Don't worry, Lotus Blossom. No one cares and they won't blame you for how I behave."

Lotus Blossom blushed, looked away, then back again. "I'm sorry, miss. But if the mistress sees that I'm not helping you, she may get angry with me."

At the maid's sorrowful face, a pang of guilt shot through Mei-hua. Lotus Blossom was right. Madam Wu would hold the maid accountable for Mei-hua's intransigence—whatever it may be—and would punish her. The punishment could be anything from a beating to dismissal. Mei-hua immediately took Lotus Blossom's hand and apologized, saying, "I won't let anything happen to you. I promise."

Lotus Blossom nodded, but Mei-hua knew she didn't fully believe her. She resolved to try and behave with more care around the compound. She didn't want any of the maids, and certainly not Lotus Blossom, to suffer because of her.

Guei-lung came up to them. "What now?"

"I think we need to discuss what we know so far before we can do anything else. Do you think we could retire to the garden without being interrupted?"

He glanced toward the gate to his mother's suite. "I heard the servants say Mother was to have guests this morning. Ping-an will probably be with them, too. No one will bother us."

She smiled. "Perfect. Let's go."

"Soldier Guo, come with us," Guei-lung ordered the young soldier, who stood nearby still holding his horse's reins.

"No. That won't be necessary," Mei-hua said quickly.

Guei-lung looked at her with a quizzical expression. She did not elaborate. Soldier Guo merely nodded; his face remained unreadable, his eyes again hidden beneath the brim of his hat as he held his head down slightly.

"All right," he amended. "You're not needed at the moment. Nevertheless, be ready in case we call you."

Guo bowed to Guei-lung's departing figure. The young man had already started toward the garden without waiting for a reply.

Mei-hua had also begun to move away with Lotus Blossom at her side. She glanced back at Guo one last time and caught his ink-black eyes flitting over to her. Although her heart ached, she held her tongue. Her trust in him appeared to have been misplaced. She resolutely turned toward the family's private quarters to meet Guei-lung and discuss the recent events. They had to report to Judge Hsu, and she didn't want Guo there to hear what she had to say.

Mei-hua and Lotus Blossom entered the garden almost immediately behind Guei-lung. As they reached the small table, he told Lotus Blossom to bring tea and whatever snacks she could find. He was hungry.

Lotus Blossom left, soon returning with a tray of delicacies. After placing the tray on the small table between them, she stood quietly to the side, ready to be of assistance. Mei-hua poured tea and Guei-lung took up his chopsticks and attacked the plate of small, steamed pockets of dough filled with various meats and fish. They sat in silence for a while as Guei-lung ate. Mei-hua stared at the gently swaying bamboo. The rustling of their leaves provided a soothing backdrop to her tangled thoughts.

Finally, having eaten several dumplings, Guei-lung laid down his chopsticks and drank his tea. Mei-hua filled his cup again and sat up on her garden stool. They discussed their trip and Mei-hua told him about Soldier Guo: about seeing him with Ching Da and his slipping away each time they visited the shops, then reappearing without a word. Guei-lung admitted that he hadn't noticed Guo's coming and going. He'd been preoccupied with each of the shopkeepers.

"Father will be pleased with this new information. As soon as court is closed for the day, we can meet with him," Guei-lung said.

"Well, while what we found out is interesting, it doesn't actually add a lot to what we already knew or suspected," Mei-hua said, shaking her head. "I think we shouldn't say anything to your father, yet."

Guei-lung let his troubled gaze rest on her for a moment. "What are you up to? What do you mean by 'yet'?"

She smiled at him. "You're so suspicious! What makes you think I'm up to something?"

He opened his eyes wide and shook his head in an exaggerated manner.

She laughed. "All right. There is something we still need to do."

"What?" He heaved an overdrawn sigh. "Although I don't even know why I asked. Whatever you're up to, it'll mean trouble."

She tipped her head and said with a grin, "All we need to do is talk to some of the other shops around the Golden Pheasant."

He groaned. "What you need to do is spend some time here at home with Mother. This is Duanwu and there's a lot to do. You should be helping with that."

Now it was Mei-hua's turn to groan. "I will, but I can't right now. We could very well miss some important information if we don't talk to some of the other nearby shopkeepers. We need to go back."

"I'll tell you what. Stay here for the rest of the day and then we can go out again tomorrow morning for another short 'shopping' trip."

Mei-hua pouted.

"Come on, Mei-hua, you have to compromise sometime. This will make Mother happy and you can still run around outside."

She rankled at his cavalier attitude, minimizing her suggestions, making it sound like what she was doing was simply playing games. But he might be right about Madam Wu. She nodded. "Promise you'll be ready to go out in the morning? If you don't, they'll never let me out of the house."

"Promise. Even though it's entirely too early for a civilized human being." He grinned.

With that settled, he told Lotus Blossom to find his servant and have his bow and arrows brought to him. He'd practice this afternoon.

Mei-hua wasn't ready to go into the confines of the women's quarters, so she stayed in the garden. Removing her tunic, she limbered up by going through the stretches Old Lin taught her. Soon she was spinning, thrusting, and parrying as she moved quickly and surely through the martial arts movements she had studied under the elderly master. It felt so good to move freely. After some time, she stopped, panting. Dark patches of sweat marred her silk blouse.

Guei-lung held his bow and watched. When she finished, he said, "You're a mess. You'd better change before Mother sees that blouse. You may have ruined the silk. If you're going to exercise, you should at least change into cotton." He frowned. "I don't know if you'll ever behave like a real lady. How will your father ever find a husband for you?"

She made a face at him, giggled, and, turning to Lotus Blossom, said, "Let's go. I'll wash up before we go see Auntie." With that she swept out of the garden, leaving Guei-lung shaking his head.

Chapter 8

THE FOLLOWING MORNING, the small procession, consisting of Mei-hua, Guei-lung, Lotus Blossom, Soldier Guo, and another guard, once more filed out of the yamen with Mei-hua and the maid in a carrier and the men riding horses. And, once more, the pretext given for their trip was shopping. They would visit the shops for Duanwu gifts. The festival and the importance of gift exchange during this time was the perfect excuse for her to be outside of the house. As with the previous morning, there were customers at the early markets wanting to purchase fresh vegetables and meats for the day. However, the crush of holiday shoppers would come later. Today Mei-hua wanted to visit stores across from the Golden Pheasant. If there was any suspicious activity, she was sure this would be the area where someone would most likely notice it.

By now, the street scene was becoming familiar. She recognized several young servants buying fruits and vegetables, vendors chatting with customers or busying themselves with their carts, and the acrobatic family. The girls tumbled and stretched in preparation for their first show of the morning. Their parents set out large, cream-colored crocks with thick, rounded sides. Soon, the girls would use these containers to balance on, as they twisted and turned their limber bodies into impossible shapes. Mei-hua watched, mesmerized, as the younger sister practiced by standing on her hands and flinging her legs straight into the air. Once stabilized, she carefully bent backwards bringing her legs out over her head and parallel to the ground. Her father watched, pointed to her legs, and called, "Don't be so lazy. Do it right."

His daughter's leg stretched out further, maintaining its parallel line to the ground. He grunted and returned to unpacking. The girl jumped down off the crock and continued stretching.

Mei-hua shook her head. She thought she was limber, but she could never bend her back like that. The girl's body was like dough—soft and pliable, able to be twisted into any shape.

The palanquin halted in front of a well-kept entrance to a prosperous looking shop that was directly across the road from the Golden Pheasant. A deeply carved placard over its entrance read: *Changsha's Gate*. Reading it, Mei-hua smiled. The name of the shop was a propitious sign. Changsha was where her father was magistrate. This merchant must come from the same western city.

Almost as soon as the carriers halted and lowered the litter, Lotus Blossom appeared at her door, ready to be of assistance. Mei-hua waved her back. They weren't at the yamen where Madam Wu would be informed of her every move. She surely didn't need help getting out of the palanquin. She proudly stuck her calamus-clad foot out the door and stepped onto the street. The entourage entered Changsha's Gate with Guei-lung leading the way, followed by Mei-hua with Lotus Blossom at her side, and Guo at the rear. The second soldier remained outside with the horses and litters. A short man in a worn—though tidy—robe scurried out from behind the counter. Clasping one hand in the other at chest level, he bowed and greeted them in a whiny, high-pitched voice.

"I would like to speak to the owner," Guei-lung said, his clear, authoritative tone a strong counter to the clerk's.

Mei-hua nodded, for she agreed with Guei-lung's apparent assumption: this person's obsequious demeanor indicated he must be a clerk. The owner of such a prosperous shop would be more confident.

"I'm sorry to say that at this moment he is unavailable. If you'll allow me, I may be of some assistance until he is free. Perhaps you'd like a cup of tea while you wait?"

"That will be fine. However, my cousin would also like to look over your merchandize," Guei-lung said.

"Of course, of course." He ordered an assistant to bring tea and indicated Guei-lung should sit at a small table to one side. Once Guei-lung was settled, he went over to Mei-hua, who was beginning to look at the shop's wares.

"Allow me to help you," he said to her.

By his accent, Mei-hua realized he wasn't native to Hangzhou. "Are you from Changsha?" she asked.

The clerk looked pleased. "Yes, indeed I am, as is the owner of Changsha's Gate. My family name is Jia."

"Ah, you are of the famous Jia lineage." Mei-hua smiled politely.

The clerk nodded, a satisfied expression crossing his face. "You have heard of the Jias. Yes. We have had many successful candidates in our family. In fact, Jia Yuan-ji, the older brother of Changsha's Gate's owner, is assistant to the Esteemed Emperor's Director of Horses."

Mei-hua immediately guessed the clerk was an extended relative of his shop's owner. By naming the important position his boss's brother held, he also was telling her that he, too, shared in the Jia family's glory.

"How fortunate your family is. The gods are smiling on you." She tried to recall what she'd learned about the different government positions. If she remembered correctly, the shop owner's brother would have been in charge of finding and maintaining herds of horses for the Emperor's military as well as for his courier network. Mei-hua wondered how long the brother had held that position, but didn't want to overstep the boundaries of casual conversation into the realm of rudeness, so she said, "By chance I traveled through Changsha with my father two years ago, but I'm sorry to say, I don't believe my father knew of Jia Yuan-ji's position or I'm sure he would have visited with him."

"Oh, the appointment is recent. Jia Yuan-ji passed the military examinations under the Yuan Dynasty, but you know how it is. With the war and change of dynasties, it took several years before he could obtain a position."

"It is a blessing our Honorable Emperor recognized his talent," Mei-hua said. "Such a position is truly a boon to your family and the community."

"Indeed. And to think it all came about through his younger brother."

Mei-hua drew her eyebrows together as if confused. "Younger brother?"

"The owner of Changsha's Gate. Jia Dou-qing is quite clever. Although the smarter of the two sons, he never cared to study and, therefore, he never sat for the examinations. Jia Dou-qing took over the family business. And, as you can see, it has grown under his care. He was able to take care of the family as well as pay for all his older brother's expenses while he studied, prepared for the examinations, and entered the bureaucracy. Between the prosperity of Changsha's Gate and the good fortune of his brother's position in the new government, the Jia family's fortunes are secure."

Mei-hua tucked away this talkative clerk's information. Now she needed to know if there was a connection between the Golden Pheasant and this shop. She looked around at the roomy interior. The counters, barrels, over-sized pots, and large sacks were all clean and neatly stacked. The floor had been swept recently. A camphor fragrance from the incense sticks burning in front of the small altar with the Buddha of Prosperity filled the spaces.

"Your shop appears to be enjoying more success than your neighbor's," she said, looking significantly out the door and toward the Golden Pheasant.

The clerk laughed. "Yes. That has a lot to do with my boss working hard—from early morning until late when all the food vendors on this street finally close for the night. The Golden Pheasant keeps irregular hours."

"I was in there the other day and bought some herbs," Mei-hua said.

"You were lucky to find it open. Although I have noticed that their doors are open more recently, perhaps in preparation for Duanwu. If they welcomed customers more, they would make a pretty copper. I've seen quite a few people come and go now that he's actually in."

"Do you know the Golden Pheasant owner well?"

"No, not really. As I say, he's seldom here and when he is, there's a lot of activity. It's a mystery to me why he doesn't stay open more often and longer, because I'm sure he'd do quite well and make lots of money." The clerk clicked his tongue and scrunched his face in bewilderment. He brightened up, "Of course, my boss, Jia Dou-qing, and he are quite friendly. They often go drinking together."

Mei-hua feigned disinterest in his comments, all the while storing each detail away to share with Magistrate Hsu. At that moment, Guei-lung came up and began engaging the clerk in conversation. They discussed the influx of tourists for the Duanwu festival and how that was good for business.

Mei-hua spied a pile of colorful threads on the back counter near a doorway from which she could hear the rumble of male voices. With a glance at Guei-lung and the clerk, who ignored her, she began slowly making her way toward the door. She carefully looked over the piles of cloth and threads laid out on one side as she did so. Some of the cloth was of the finest brocade in either bright or subdued colors. All beautiful. In honor of the festival, there were a couple of bolts of cloth with the *wudu*—the five poisonous animals—embroidered on them: the tiger, toad, snake, scorpion, and centipede. Most of the brocades were embellished with clouds, flowers, and vases, all of which were good luck symbols. As she moved toward the back, she ran her fingers over the materials, luxuriating in their smoothness.

Not far from the doorway, three over-sized dishes sat on the counter. They held popular Duanwu gifts. One bowl held ropes of intertwined five-colored silk threads that girls wore in their hair. Another dish almost over-flowed with five-colored silk bracelets. And an array of dainty sachets with five-colored threads sewn across their openings, in order to tie the bags shut, filled the final plate.

She stood examining each of these piles while Guei-lung distracted the clerk. Mei-hua surveyed the area and located Guo standing in a corner, eyes ever roving around the room, as if keeping a lookout for danger. His gaze swept toward her; their eyes met and held. His glance only confused her more. She looked away and down at the ribbon of color resting in her hand. *How could he betray them*? The question had become a mantra, playing over and over in her mind. A heaviness settled in her chest.

As she strolled closer to the back of the store, she heard voices. They came from a back room and, while muted, they were distinct enough to understand. She laid three, multi-colored ribbons on the counter, as if comparing them to decide which looked best, and tried to look natural as she strained to make out the conversation.

"We have to get moving. Have you seen to the boats and carts?"

"We need 350 boats and probably more than 500 carts. There's no way people aren't going to notice our moving the goods out of here. Why do you want to do it now, during Duanwu, when there are so many extra sets of eyes in town?"

"You're such a fool. We're not greedy. We're not going to steal the whole shipment. Of course tea and the brocades have to be exchanged for horses. We'll only take twenty percent of the goods for our trouble."

A burst of laughter, followed by coughing, interrupted the conversation.

"You'd better do something about that cough."

"I have my mugwort and calamus talisman. I'll be fine." His cough ended in a spasm this time.

"You ought to be drinking realgar wine to stop your hacking. Now that it's Duanwu, it's much easier to find than at any other time of the year."

"Good idea. I'll get some from our friend in the Western Branch." He coughed again, then Mei-hua heard a spurt of spit. "Still, why move the goods now, when the city is so busy?"

"If we take our cut before the trade goods leave on their journey, we'll have a hard time getting them out without the guards at the city gates noticing. This way, we can move them with the official government convoy of goods in the tea-horse trade. And, because there is so much going on now and the place is overly full, the guards are not being very careful about their duties. Due to their distraction, and, of course, with a few extra coppers for their efforts, they will report the numbers I give them when they fill out the forms for merchandize being transported out of the city. Once we're out and safely in the countryside, we can divert the boats and carts without attracting undue attention.

"Go bring us some wine." The scraping of stools being moved around alerted Mei-hua. She abruptly turned away from the door, holding up two of the five-colored silk bracelets she had been examining. With her head pointed toward the bracelets, she peered sideways to see who came out of the room. Almost instantaneously, a gnarled, balding man wearing a short jacket tied at the waist, pushed out of the back room. He stopped abruptly when he saw Mei-hua standing nearby at the counter and stared at her.

As if unaware of his presence, she took up another bracelet, slipped it on her wrist, and held it up to the light. Her eyes frantically searched out Soldier Guo, who no longer stood in the corner. The clumping of boots on wood told of Guo's approach. The bald man retreated into the back room. A rush of voices too low to understand gushed through the door. She didn't know exactly what the rough looking fellow said, but she could guess. He'd spotted her listening in on their conversation. However, she hoped, if they regarded her as a mere girl, they'd ignore her as someone who was ignorant and harmless.

Guo stopped behind her. She immediately grabbed several multi-colored bracelets and hair ribbons, then promptly moved to where Guei-lung and the clerk were talking.

"Ah, my lady, I see you have chosen some of our most beautiful pieces." The clerk smiled widely and took them from her. "Let me wrap these. And as a special gift, I will include a fragrant sachet for you to wear during Duanwu."

"These are lovely, Mei-hua. Who did you buy them for?" Guei-lung asked.

"For Gran'ma Fei, Auntie Xi and our cousins," Mei-hua said.

"Have you finished shopping? Or, do you want to visit another shop, nearby perhaps?" Guei-lung asked.

Since she was sure the thugs in the back at least suspected she'd heard their conversation, she wondered if she should hurry back to the safety of the compound. They were now standing at the entrance of Changsha's Gate. Mei-hua scrutinized the growing crowds. She'd already learned quite a bit, returning now would be the smartest thing to do. She was about to tell Guei-lung that she wanted to go home when she saw two figures exit the Golden Phoenix.

"Look, across the street," she said. She leaned into Lotus Blossom and lightly touched her arm pretending to talk to her, while pointing in the direction of the street.

Guei-lung squinted toward the exposed doorway and the men. His eyes widened. A man, who could only be described as a thug, was leaving the Golden Phoenix with a familiar figure. Ching Da.

Chapter 9

THE TWO MEN walked purposefully out into the street and stood together briefly in an excited exchange.

Mei-hua shot a sidewise glance at Soldier Guo. He appeared to be looking up the street in the opposite direction. Had he seen Ching Da? Mei-hua wanted to follow the gang leader, but should Guo go with them? She had to decide, and quickly.

"Soldier Guo," she called out. He briskly responded, coming to her side. Energy oozed around him, creating a zone of vitality Mei-hua found as attractive as his black dancing eyes. She stepped away from him and closer to Guei-lung.

"Soldier Guo," she repeated in a more subdued voice, "go to Magistrate Hsu's office and tell him we've just seen Ching Da at the Golden Pheasant again."

"Won't you be returning? I should accompany you back to the compound," he said, hovering over her, feet firmly apart. "It's not safe for you to be out here. You should be home." His hand opened and closed on his weapon.

Mei-hua immediately chafed at his presumption in speaking to her like this, as if giving her an order. *You should be home.* It was too much. Mei-hua threw her head back. "I'll decide what is best for me."

Guo's hand clutched his weapon, but he dropped his head and said in a softer voice, "Forgive me. I didn't mean to offend you. I was merely pointing out that Master Hsu and Madam Wu would feel better if you were safely within their residence's walls."

Mei-hua shook her head. "I want to visit a couple more shops, and Magistrate Hsu should learn of the gang leader's presence as soon as possible." She glanced over at the other young soldier accompanying them. "Besides, I still have this guard and Guei-lung. You must tell the honorable magistrate about Ching Da immediately." She tried to diffuse his concern by grinning and adding, "That's more important than my shopping. Really, what could go wrong when I'll have them with me?"

Guo's lips tightened into a frown and he seemed about to comment. Then he merely gave her a small bow and said, "As you wish." Without pause, he strode to his horse, jumped on its back, and rode away, leaving them in a whirl of dust.

"Why did you do that?" Guei-lung asked, perplexed. He waved a hand in front of his face, trying to dispel the engulfing dirt. Then, "Oh, does this have to do with what we talked about in the garden?"

"Yes, I don't want him to know too much about what we are about to do."

"About to do? What are we about to do?" Guei-lung asked.

Mei-hua again indicated that he should look across the busy street. Ching Da and his accomplice were still engaged in an intense discussion. Ching Da abruptly stopped gesturing wildly and, after a brief check of the area, marched toward the warehouse district with the thug trotting briskly behind him, trying to keep up.

"We're must follow them," she said, climbing into the palanquin. "Lotus Blossom, get into your litter. Don't delay."

Then, to the carriers, "Quickly, take me down to the warehouse district.

"Guei-lung, don't lose them. We'll be right behind." She adjusted her curtain to allow her to stick her head out while keeping the curtain close to her face. In this way, she was able to keep an eye on Guei-lung. Even amongst the crowds he wasn't difficult to see, since he was on a horse and the revelers filling the streets were on foot.

Guei-lung ordered the soldier to stay with her and he rode his horse on ahead.

Ching Da and his companion sped along through the crowd; Guei-lung warily followed. The two men appeared to be unconcerned about being seen. They moved deliberately and without caution down the bustling main street until they reached the warehouse district. Once there, they entered a narrower, but still busy, avenue. Guei-lung paused, allowing Mei-hua's guard to see him enter before he ventured after the thugs.

Shortly, however, the men came to an alley and pushed through a cluster of merrymakers blocking its entrance. Guei-lung slowly approached, stopped, and watched as they disappeared. He dismounted and waited for Mei-hua to catch up.

As soon as her litter arrived, she pushed its curtain completely back and out of the way. A flood of light spewed into the tiny compartment.

"Where are they? What are they doing?" she asked as she stuck her head out the window.

"They just went into that nearby warehouse. The second one on the right." Guei-lung pointed into the alley. A large, ramshackle building spread out over an entire block, throwing a deep shadow over the front passageway. There were no workers outside. Indeed, now that they were on a side street and no longer in the shopping district, the roads were almost empty and only a few idlers meandered through the alley. Although hidden by the enormous building, they could smell the moist air coming from the river that ran behind it.

Mei-hua jumped out of the litter. "Follow us, but stay behind, unless you're needed," she told the guard, who nodded.

"We've got to find out what he's up to. Now may be our best chance," she said to Guei-lung.

"Don't you think we should wait for Soldier Guo?" he asked nervously.

"Wait for Soldier Guo?" She turned to Guei-lung in surprise. "He's not coming. Remember, I told him to report to your father. He doesn't even know where we are, which was the point of sending him away. We don't know if we can trust him. And now isn't the time to find out." She frowned. Then looked down the alley toward the doorway Ching Da entered.

"Lotus Blossom, stay where you are," she ordered her maid, who was about to descend from her palanquin.

Lotus Blossom protested. "I must stay with you, Mistress. I won't be in the way; I'll only be where you need me."

"I need you to stay where you are," Mei-hua said. She understood Lotus Blossom's desire to protect her, but she was getting tired of everyone wanting to care for her by stifling her. "We'll be right back. Stay. Here. Do you understand?"

Lotus Blossom nodded her head and moved back into the litter, still frowning.

Mei-hua spun around on her heel. "Let's go," she said to Guei-lung and hurried into the darkened alley.

Guei-lung sighed but followed, indicating the guard should stay close behind.

They stealthily approached the warehouse. A fresh, slightly astringent fragrance accosted them as they came up to the front door, which stood ajar. Mei-hua stepped forward and peered inside. Mounds of bales of tea ran along the walls and sat in clusters throughout the warehouse. From the refreshing scent, Mei-hua realized that they were in fact surrounded by the best tea produced in southern China, ready to be moved west and traded on behalf of the Emperor for horses. In stark contrast to the vacant roads outside, the interior of the warehouse crawled with men. Laborers bustled around, some moving goods toward large, gaping doors, others dragging carts into the middle of the storeroom's expansive floor.

Ching Da stood in the center, calling out orders. He directed some laborers to place bales of tea onto boats waiting just outside the warehouse; other men he ordered to load another set of bales—marked with a different symbol—onto the carts.

"What are they loading?" Guei-lung whispered into her ear.

She stared into the dusky interior, straining to see the markings painted on their sides. "Brocades," she said. "To be traded along with the tea."

"Why isn't he sending them all by boat? It'd be faster," Guei-lung said.

"Maybe they're too precious and susceptible to damage if wet. River water is filthy. Filled with silt. It would ruin silk brocades if they got wet, and I doubt they could move up-river through some of the narrow passageways without the turbulent water getting onto the boats."

"But wouldn't that be true for the tea as well?" Guei-lung said, straining to see over the top of Mei-hua's head.

"You're right." She shrugged her shoulders. "I don't know. Maybe the goods are going to different locations."

"Hmm."

Before he could say more, Mei-hua poked him and pointed into the corner of the enormous building. A fierce dragon raised its massive head.

"Ah," Guei-lung exhaled in admiration.

They both gaped at the apparition. Intense, angry eyes pierced through the dimness. With flaring nostrils, its gold and jade-green head stretched forward to conquer space. Even the murky gloom of the warehouse couldn't hide the glow of the golden scales covering its long body. Its tail resembled a fire igniting the dragon and pushing it onward.

For a brief moment, they were overcome by the creature's ferocious beauty and strength; their minds struggled to understand what they were seeing. As Mei-hua stared at the vision, she became aware of movement near the dragon. A small contingent of men slowly moved around the beast's body, painstakingly painting each scale along the dragon's side.

The workers were turning a teakwood boat into a glowing dragon masterpiece. A dragon boat. The race was just days away and this beauty would certainly be one of the most magnificent on the water. It was a long boat, big enough for a dozen or two rowers, a drummer to keep the rowing rhythm—and the all important flag bearer. The flag identified the village, business, or clan that owned the vessel.

A crash followed by an explosion of curses from within the warehouse made Mei-hua and Guei-lung jump. They quickly scrambled away from the open door to avoid being seen by anyone inside. A barrage of angry voices, stomping boots, and wood scraping over the rock-hard floor burst into the alley. Mei-hua furtively returned and looked around the door jam. The dragon boat had slipped off its support and was leaning heavily to one side, threatening to complete its fall onto the unforgiving floor. A mass of men swarmed around it, adjusting the supports and struggling to hoist it up and reset it on the wooden trusses.

"What are you waiting for? Go out and get the lever! You'll never get that thing back up if you don't," Ching Da yelled. Men ran out the immense, yawning door in the back wall and onto the adjoining wharf. He started toward the alley's door. "Make sure it's ready for the race. We don't want to disappoint the boss," he called to them.

Afraid he was about to come in their direction, Mei-hua and Guei-lung fled back to the palanquin and horse before they could be seen. As she reached her litter, Mei-hua cast one last glance down the alley toward the warehouse. At that moment, Ching Da erupted from the building, arms flailing, yelling and cursing at the workers.

Wasting no more time, Mei-hua leaped into the litter. The carriers plunged into the crowded street as the soldier created an opening for them. Mei-hua sat against the litter's hard, wood back. The sharp sounds of bargaining in the market—mixed with the rhythmic drum beat of the acrobats' routine—soon replaced Ching Da's hoarse voice.

Barely noticing the litter's fluttering turquoise curtains that protected her from the dust rising from the street, Mei-hua replayed the scene with Ching Da. He had referred to "the boss," which had to mean he wasn't the ultimate leader of this gang. How was she going to find out who was behind the theft of the tea-horse trade cargo, the person who was out to destroy her father?

Chapter 10

MEI-HUA HAD HOPED they could return unnoticed to the Hsu compound. However, it was now early afternoon and she was sure Madam Wu would have realized they weren't home for lunch. How could she explain not only why they were out again but also why they were so late? Shopping would not be accepted as a reason, she was sure.

Lotus Blossom had just pulled back the curtain on the palanquin's door to allow Mei-hua to exit when several servants came rushing out from Madam Wu's suite. They formed a small line and waited in silence for her to descend from the litter. Mei-hua sighed. It looked like she was in trouble. Again. She took Lotus Blossom's hand and descended from the litter with as much grace as she could muster. She glanced at Guei-lung, who had dismounted. One of Madam Wu's attendants was talking to him; he looked grim. Finally, he nodded and walked towards Mei-hua.

"Mother wants to see us right away. We're not even to go and clean up after being out on the street," he said when he reached her.

                                                  P.A. De Voe

Mei-hua tried to maintain a calm face, but couldn't keep from grimacing slightly.

"Yes, I know. I'm sure she's not happy with us," he said.

With us? Mei-hua thought. *Or with me?*

"Don't mention Ching Da or the warehouse," Mei-hua whispered. "We'll tell your father, but your mother may react badly."

"You know she'll find out eventually. Father will tell her. She may already know because we sent Guo back to say we saw Ching Da," he said in a low voice so the attendants wouldn't hear. She shot a guilty look at him. Sending Guo back had been her idea. He'd opposed it, and now that act was promising to be another nail in their coffin. Mei-hua had really gotten him into double trouble. She was sorry, but she'd had to do it. There had been no other choice.

"One thing at a time. We don't know if your father will tell her. He may consider it to be a secret. He doesn't share his work with her, so she may never learn about it. Let's only talk about the shopping," Mei-hua stated in as confident a manner as she could. She hoped what she said with such assurance would actually be true.

Guei-lung merely shook his head.

Lotus Blossom's shadow crossed in front of them as they started toward Madam Wu's chambers. Mei-hua stopped. "Lotus Blossom, do you have the packages I bought at Changsha's Gate?"

"Yes, Mistress." She took out two small packages from her sleeves and handed them to Mei-hua. "Here they are."

Mei-hua took them and smiled at Guei-lung. "At least we did buy something to show that we'd been shopping."

He rolled his eyes. "Come on. Let's get this over with."

Clutching the packages as if they were talismans to protect against disaster, she followed Guei-lung into the lion's den. A mugwort figure and a picture of the ghost chaser, hung from Madam Wu's outer door. The refreshingly sweet scent of seasonal flowers cleansed the room's air. Ping-an sat on the kang, impeccable and luminous in a pale gold skirt, green blouse, and lavender over-jacket. Mei-hua was painfully aware of her own dusty clothes as she came forward and stood before the silent, stern figure sitting next to her friend. Dressed in her embroidered brocades of blues and reds, Madam Wu was no less radiant than her daughter, albeit far more intimidating.

"Good afternoon, Mother. I hope you are well today," Guei-lung said with his most charming smile.

"Good afternoon, Auntie," Mei-hua murmured, bowing deeply.

Madam Wu glared at the two before her. Finally, turning her full attention toward Mei-hua, she fairly hissed, "What do you think you were doing? How could you betray Master Hsu's trust in you so badly? He gave you permission to go out to shop when Guei-lung and guards accompanied you."

"I..." Mei-hua started.

"Don't interrupt me, young lady. You are a young woman from a distinguished family and will behave properly. When Master Hsu said you could go outside the compound, he didn't mean you could leave the women's quarters without letting me know where you were going and when. He didn't mean you could wander about every day." She leaned forward. "And then what do I find out? Not only have you gone outside without my permission, but you sent back one of your guards, leaving only a single soldier with you." She straightened her shoulders and sat up. "That is in direct disobedience with Master Hsu's orders."

"But, Mother..." Guei-lung started.

"And you, young man," she glared at her son, "Just what were you thinking? How dare you be so careless as to not let me know what she was doing? How could you send that guard back? You're as bad as she is."

"Father did say Mei-hua could go outside the compound. Perhaps we misjudged how often," Guei-lung managed to get in, trying to ameliorate his mother's anger.

"Master Hsu," his mother used this formal address for his father when she was really angry, "did not give permission for wanton behavior and disregard for propriety," she stormed.

"It's only because this is Duanwu and Mei-hua wanted to do special shopping. Otherwise, I'm sure she wouldn't go out so often," he inserted quickly.

"Shopping! We have servants for that," his mother returned. Then, again giving Mei-hua her full attention, she said, "And just what did you buy, if anything?"

Mei-hua opened her hand and held out the two little packages, now quite crushed as she had unwittingly held them in a death-grip throughout Madam Wu's tirade. Her Aunt told a servant to bring her the bundles for inspection.

Opening the mashed packages, she held up the multi-colored ribbons and bracelets. "Who are these for? Why did you purchase them?"

"I understood that we would be visiting Gran'ma Fei, Auntie Xi, and our cousins tomorrow, and I had no Duanwu gifts for them." Since Madam Wu appeared to be listening, Mei-hua quickly continued. "When we left this morning, I had no idea it would take us so long. I am deeply sorry to have caused so much worry and trouble for you, Auntie," she said, bowing again, eyes on the floor.

Madam Wu settled back against the brilliant blue cushions behind her. She gave the trinkets to her maid and waved a hand, directing her to return the gifts to Mei-hua. "Yes, that is good."

Mei-hua's body began to relax. She had almost allowed herself to stretch her shoulders when Madam Wu went on. "It's still not an excuse to leave the compound without letting me know or not keeping the appropriate number of guards—the number Master Hsu required—when you're out." Although her words continued to chastise Mei-hua, the tone had softened considerably. Having Duanwu gifts to exchange with relatives was important and a sign of respect.

Mei-hua felt a rush of relief. She was grateful for all Madam Wu and her husband had done for her, and did not relish disobeying them. At the same time, she had her own path to follow. She had to help her father, to find out who was trying to incriminate him and to destroy her family.

"Nevertheless, what you did was wrong and dangerous," Madam Wu went on. "You are my responsibility, not just to keep you alive and well, but also to protect your reputation as a young woman in society. Master Hsu had given you permission to go out with at least two guards, and since you've betrayed this trust, I am now forbidding you from leaving the compound or even the women's quarters. You will not have to seek out anymore gifts. If you have any needs, anything at all, let me know. I will tend to them. You needn't concern yourself about anything that would take you beyond the yamen's walls."

Mei-hua's shoulders dropped. She kept her eyes down, now as much to hide her disappointment as to show respect. So she was to be imprisoned once again!

"Orchid," Madam Wu turned to a maid standing closest to her. "I want you to accompany Mei-hua and take care of her. You are also to report to me on how she is doing."

Mei-hua felt a hot flush rise up from her neck and into her face. The real purpose behind Madam Wu's giving Orchid—a senior maid—to Mei-hua was obvious: she would keep her mistress informed on whatever Mei-hua did. Now she had two people spying on her: Soldier Guo and Orchid!

"You may return to your chambers, Mei-hua. Guei-lung, go study. You've been neglecting your lessons for too long and your father will be displeased." With that, she dismissed the two recalcitrant youths.

Bowing low, Mei-hua and Guei-lung escaped together. Outside the door, before Guei-lung turned away to go to his rooms, she murmured, "I can still go into the garden. Go practice your archery in the bamboo grove. I'll see you as soon as I can."

He nodded and left.

Mei-hua kept her head high as she plodded back to her rooms with Lotus Blossom and Orchid following behind her. Before she could step inside, a rustle of silks and the delicate scent of jasmine alerted her to Ping-an's presence. She paused and shifted to the outside of the veranda's walkway, allowing Ping-an to join her.

"Such bad luck to be in trouble with Mama," Ping-an said. "Now you'll have to remain in the compound, as well."

Mei-hua thought she caught a trace of satisfaction in her friend's voice.

"She wants to protect me," Mei-hua said.

"Well, being inside isn't so bad. We'll be together. There are so many things to do. But, of course, it's not as bad as Mama made it seem. We'll still be able to go out of the house—when we visit Auntie Xi's to celebrate Double Fifth Day and the dragon boat race," Ping-an added consolingly. "So it's not like you have to stay in all the time."

Mei-hua looked out into the courtyard's garden and grimaced. She didn't want Ping-an to see her face. She was being imprisoned by those who loved her and wanted only what they thought was best for her. Nevertheless, she silently fumed. Keeping her locked away in the Hsu compound wasn't what she needed. She walked along with Ping-an in silence, and soon her cousin also became quiet. As they were about to enter their rooms, they heard a soft *thwack, thwack* sound, followed quickly by another *thwack, thwack*.

Ping-an's brows drew together in a quizzical look. "Guei-lung is practicing his archery. He's so much better at memorizing the Confucian classics and writing essays than he is at shooting his bow. I wonder why he's practicing now. It usually aggravates him even more." She peered in the direction of the garden.

"Let's go to the bamboo grove and watch," Mei-hua said.

Ping-an laughed guilelessly. "Yes, he could use a break even before he's begun." Her laughter rippled through the courtyard's still air. Leaning on Mei-hua and a maid for support, she glided along around the veranda and through the gate into the bamboo garden.

As they entered the grove, they saw Guei-lung and his attendants through the bamboo. Before the girls could alert him to their presence, he'd already recognized them approaching. He handed his bow to the nearby servant carrying his arrows.

"Bring tea, steamed *baozi* filled with seafood, and fruit," he ordered another maid standing to the side.

"Come. We can drown our bad luck in tea and smother our sorrow in snacks," he ended with a broad bow.

"Now you two will understand how I feel, always being confined to the house and gardens," Ping-an said.

"But I thought you liked it," Guei-lung protested.

She stuck her tongue out at him. "That was when I was a child. I'm older now."

"And in greater need to be watched over," he returned.

"I'm the same age as Mei-hua and you don't think she needs to be kept behind closed doors," Ping-an pouted.

Guei-lung picked up a baozi the servant had placed on a table near them. Taking a big bite, he nodded and chewed vigorously. "But she's not afraid of anything. And she's competent."

"What? I'm not competent?" Ping-an gasped. "I may not act like a boy, but I can take care of myself."

The insult of suggesting she was like a boy hit Mei-hua hard. It was obvious Ping-an was hurt and angry and taking her feelings out on them. *Was she going to lose Ping-an's friendship because of jealousy?* she worried. It wasn't Mei-hua's fault Madam Wu was bound and determined to protect them in the most traditional and time-sanctioned way—by controlling their movements and their freedom—and Ping-an's misplaced anger struck her as unfair. Even so, the girls' friendship meant a lot to Mei-hua, and the thought of being without it troubled her as much as the loss of her freedom.

Chapter 11

THE DAY STARTED OFF with rain and wind, a combination that increased the air's penetrating chill. The coolness of spring fought against giving way to the warmth of summer. Mei-hua slipped on a heavy cotton vest festooned with butterflies. Burning wood infused the room with a comforting smell as the fire under the kang warmed the girls. Mei-hua and Ping-an sat with their legs tucked under them and shared a shimmering silk quilt embroidered with large, yellow and white chrysanthemums. They had pulled the quilt over their laps, trapping the kang's rising heat.

An attendant placed a low, rectangular table in front of them on the kang. Mei-hua eyed the small dishes of cold vegetables and the plate of steamed dumplings filled with lotus paste. Cold food on what promised to be a long, cold day. She had little enthusiasm for breakfast. Melodious notes of Ping-an's song bird broke through her trance-like state. She glanced over at the tiny, brown warbler singing with all its might from inside a lacquered cage just big enough for the tiny bird to hop from one perch to the other. Mei-hua closed her eyes. That was her: well taken care of, but a prisoner nonetheless.

Ping-an had been chatting non-stop. Tomorrow they would all be going over to Auntie Xi's. She was excited about what she would wear, what games they would play, what favorite Duanwu foods they would eat on their picnic, and how exciting the dragon boat race would be. If only they could see it and not just hear about what happened. All the while, Mei-hua sat glumly watching the little bird, not paying much attention. Finally, Ping-an stopped. She threw her arms around Mei-hua and hugged her tightly.

"Don't be sad. We'll have fun; we'll be together," Ping-an said, giving her another squeeze. "Aren't you happy here?"

Mei-hua tried to grin at her friend, but could not prevent some sadness from reaching her eyes. "Of course. You and your family have been very kind, better than I deserve." She looked toward the veranda, hoping to pull Ping-an's attention away from her and towards the weather outside. "Pay no attention to me. It's this rainy day, that's all," Mei-hua lied.

Well, she thought, *the first part was true.* Ping-an's family had been very good to her. But she was deeply depressed by the turn of events. Being the daughter of such a household certainly had advantages: clothing, food, shelter, and education—of a sort. But it also had disadvantages. If she were a poor farmer's daughter, she would have more freedom. Not as much as a boy of any social class would have, but more than this beautifully lacquered cage allowed her.

"If you aren't going to eat anything, we should go and pay our morning respects to Mother," Ping-an said. "After that, we can read."

Mei-hua almost smiled. Ping-an still did not care much for reading, but she knew how much Mei-hua enjoyed the hours spent with her head in a book.

"I'm ready," Mei-hua said as the maids removed the breakfast table from their kang.

Madam Wu was in a much better mood than yesterday. When the girls entered, she smiled broadly and invited them to sit on the kang with her. "It's warmer over here than in a chair, and I can tell you about our plans for visiting your Auntie Xi," she said.

Ping-an settled down on her right side and Mei-hua sat next to Ping-an. Madam Wu's maids were about to cover their legs with a silk quilt when Guei-lung entered for his morning greeting. After bowing to his mother, he remained standing, ready to receive any instructions she would have for him.

"Spend the day wisely, Guei-lung. Tomorrow you will be excused from studying because we'll all go to Auntie Xi's to celebrate and you can go to the dragon boat races."

"Yes, Mother," he said.

"Now go study," she said.

However, before he left, a messenger from Master Hsu's office entered. The judge wanted to see Mei-hua and Guei-lung in the office as soon as they'd finished their morning greeting. Ping-an pouted and frowned. Madam Wu pulled her shoulders back and sat straighter. Irritation at the request oozed from her posture, but she simply said, "Yes, of course. They can attend to him immediately.

"Guei-lung, escort Mei-hua to your father's office. You can both return here once you've finished," she said.

Mei-hua scrambled off the kang and fairly dashed to Guei-lung's side.

"Proceed as a young lady should," Madam Wu said, a reprimand coloring her words, thereby creating a stronger rebuke.

Mei-hua stopped, bowed in her direction, and proceeded to accompany Guei-lung out of the room—at an unhurried, deliberate pace. However, as soon as they stepped onto the veranda spread across the front of her suite, the two nearly flew to the judge's office. At his door, they paused to steady their breathing before entering.

Judge Hsu wore the floor-length, grey robe and the simple hat of a scholar, rather than his official magistrate robes and black gauze hat with its rounded wings on either side. He intently studied a long sheet of paper unrolled to the width of his desk. The scrape of ink stick against ink stone drew Mei-hua's attention. The judge's secretary sat at a table under a window writing up the many reports required to be sent to the capital.

Mei-hua and Guei-lung bowed and remained standing.

"Come closer to the desk," the judge ordered. His dark, hooded eyes revealed no hint of what he was thinking. His face was grave.

Mei-hua came forward with measured dignity and stood before him with Guei-lung. She braced herself for bad news, as nothing about the judge indicated he had anything good to tell them.

"I wasn't able to meet with you earlier because I was kept late by court events, but now I want to know what happened when you two went into the market. Soldier Guo reported rather early to me, saying that you'd seen Ching Da. Yet, with such a dangerous person about, you sent back one of your two guards. Explain yourselves."

Mei-hua shifted from one foot to the other. Guei-lung cleared his throat and placed one hand behind his back, as if to recite his lessons.

"When we were in Changsha's Gate, we saw Ching Da come out of the shop across the street with another man. They were arguing. Ching Da shoved his finger hard into the other man's chest. Nevertheless, the other guy kept on arguing," Guei-lung said.

"Could you hear what it was about?"

"No, they were too far away and the street noise was too loud."

The judge nodded. "Continue."

"Mei-hua—we—thought you should learn of his presence immediately, so we sent Soldier Guo on ahead...and we came later."

The judge rubbed his eyes, then slowly let his gaze rest fully on Mei-hua. "Why Soldier Guo and why then?"

Mei-hua shifted her weight once more and swallowed. She hoped her nervousness wasn't too apparent.

"Start at the beginning, Mei-hua. First, why did you go to Changsha's Gate? I'm sure it wasn't simply to shop."

Standing erect with one hand behind her back, she began. "We suspected, from our previous trip to the Golden Pheasant and the Western Branch, that there was suspicious activity going on in that area. We'd seen Ching Da in the vicinity earlier as well, so it seemed worthwhile to check into the situation a bit more. We hoped the merchant across from the Golden Pheasant would have observed something of note. So," she hurried on, "we went to Changsha's Gate as if shopping for Duanwu gifts, but really to get more information on the merchant and his clerks. Unlike the Golden Pheasant, Changsha's Gate is a prosperous store, kept in good condition. The fact that it attracts many customers shows that the location is a good place for a business—if it's an honest establishment with an owner who wants people in his store."

"You think the Golden Pheasant is a front." It was not a question.

"Yes. Apparently, the owner is wealthy with a large home and a concubine, yet his store is abysmal—dirty, poorly lit, with old and neglected goods. No customers came in while we were there and we never did see anyone entering it— except for Ching Da and his thug."

"What did you find out from Changsha's Gate's owner?"

"A couple of things, which really confirm what we already guessed. First, he and his clerks observed very few customers going into the Golden Pheasant, and those they had seen sounded like Ching Da and his thugs. They didn't come by randomly, but seemed to arrive in a group every few days." She paused.

"Go on."

Keeping her eyes on his chin, she continued. "The merchant at Changsha's Gate said its owner actually came from Changsha, where his family was one of the most distinguished in the district. They own a lot of land and his brother, Jia Yuan-ji, had passed the government exams to the third level. He held a position as assistant to the Director of Horses."

"Ah," Judge Hsu said. "So, this merchant is of the Jia family. That both explains some things and causes problems. But never mind. We'll get to that later."

Guei-lung jumped in. "It's after getting that information that we saw Ching Da."

"Which gets us back to why you sent Soldier Guo to me with such information, leaving you exposed."

Mei-hua felt his gaze burrowing into her.

"You don't trust him," the judge said. "Because of our earlier conversation."

"Yes. If he were a spy—and it surely looks like he is—as well as a friend of Ching Da's, I didn't want him with us. The only way to get rid of him, without causing misgiving, was to send him to you with that message," she said. "I still had the guard with me," she hastily added. "And, of course, Guei-lung."

She could feel the young man beside her stand taller.

"Yes, she was well protected," Guei-lung said.

"I understand why you sent him back, but you were being extremely foolish. Did Ching Da see you in Changsha's Gate?"

"No, I don't think so. They seemed to be quite involved in their discussion. And, even when they went to the warehouse, they never seemed concerned about being followed," Guei-lung said.

His father glared from one to the other. "You followed them to a warehouse?"

Guei-lung, seeming to realize he'd said too much, blushed and stared at his feet.

"Mei-hua, explain and don't try to hide anything from me," Judge Hsu ordered.

Mei-hua felt warmth creep into her cheeks. She hadn't meant to hide their activities from him. His support was necessary for her to have any modicum of freedom. Certainly, Madam Wu would never let her out of the women's quarters if it were up to her. She had to have the judge on her side. It was just that she had gotten focused on what she thought had to be investigated and, well, forgot.

"Honorable Uncle," she began, "when we went to the street and the shops, it wasn't our intent to break any rules or to do anything dangerous. Not that we did anything dangerous," she hurriedly added. "When we saw Ching Da, we thought it would be a good idea to follow him and see if he would lead us to anything of importance. He could have just gone to a wine house, but even that might have been useful information, because then we'd know something about his habits." Mei-hua hoped this made sense and was acceptable to the judge.

"How did you follow him if you were in your palanquin?"

"Guei-lung was on horseback, so he went on ahead and kept track of Ching Da. My carriers moved quickly, keeping his horse within eyesight."

"Good thinking, as far as it went," the judge said. "But a litter following behind someone is hard to miss."

"They didn't seem to be the least concerned about anyone following them," Guei-lung repeated. "They never looked behind them. I was careful," he said. "We followed them to a warehouse full of bales of tea and brocades. At least that's how the bales were marked. Apparently, they were getting ready to transfer the goods out west as part of the tea-horse trade."

The judge stroked his beard in thought. Then, "Anything else? Anything else of interest?"

Mei-hua paused before adding, "There was also a dragon boat in the building; it was being painted in preparation for the competition on Double Fifth Day," she said, using the familiar term for the day of the Dragon Boat Festival.

The judge leaned forward; a flash of interest crossed his face. "Were you able to discover who owns the boat?"

"No, there was no placard or flag with the owner's name. But I'm sure we would recognize it again if we see it at the races," she said.

Judge Hsu leaned back into his ornately carved chair. "You two have done well," he said, then added, "although you should never have gone off like that. In the future..."

Mei-hua stiffened, prepared to be condemned to remain forever in the compound or Aunt Xi's home.

"...I want you to keep Soldier Guo with you," he said.

Mei-hua finally began to relax. Yet, as her tension lifted, confusion filled in the empty space. Guo was a spy. Of that she was certain, for she'd seen him with the gang leader herself. Then the constant underlying question became even more important: should they let him stay so close? He could betray them at any moment, putting them in real danger.

"You're wondering about Guo, I'm sure," Hsu said, as if reading her mind. "The fact that they found you here in my home, Mei-hua, before Soldier Guo's arrival, shows that there's an extensive network even without him. Plus, as long as he's with you and is under my supervision, I don't think he would do something against you. Spy on you and report to his uncle, the eunuch, yes, but not overtly break his duty to me and, thereby, to the empire." He pushed back against the chair once more. "They—whoever *they* are—probably already know you followed Ching Da and you've found the warehouse. We must be careful."

Mei-hua felt hope surge through her. He had said, "We."

"In the meantime, rest today. Do what Madam Wu says," he grinned, then added, "and tomorrow we'll all go to the home of my mother-in-law and sister-in-law to share in celebrating Duanwu.

"Mei-hua," he said, his voice now more tender, "I've heard from your father. He's currently working with a local elite in his prefecture to resolve the problem. As you know, bringing a case against a member of a distinguished family, if that should prove to be the case, is complicated. There are laws protecting those who've passed the national examinations. Bringing them before a court of law is fraught with difficulty, if not impossible.

On the other hand, if we're simply dealing with Ching Da and other gangsters like him, it will be a lot easier to bring the case to court and to find him guilty. We'll have to wait to hear more about what is happening in Changsha. In the meantime, I will keep an eye on Ching Da and his gang. We can look for the dragon boat you saw in the warehouse. That may lead us to others in the gang."

He nodded and dismissed them with a wave. "You may go now. Study, rest, and enjoy the holiday. I will have my men keep an eye on our thugs."

Mei-hua bowed deeply before him. "Uncle, I don't mean to bother you with my insignificant problems, but, if you would be so kind, I have a request."

He stared at her. "Go on."

"My esteemed Aunt..."

"Ah, yes. She discussed the question of your behavior with me last night. You know she's quite upset. She's responsible for you and is accountable to your father." He peered at her. "She's not accustomed to young ladies challenging her or running about outside the protection of their homes—even with guards." A slight twitch at the corner of his mouth made Mei-hua think he'd smile, but he didn't. "Neither am I.

"But, you are your father's daughter. I find I am walking a fine line between allowing you the privileges and freedom, within limits, he would allow you and, at the same time, ensuring your safety—both from thugs and from unsavory gossip."

What was this leading up to? She so wanted him to once more give her permission to move about, even with Guei-lung, a maid, and guards.

She didn't have long to wait for his position.

"Don't worry. I'll talk with her. We can work things out. As I've said before, a mother, even a surrogate mother, is like a tiger and will protect her young. Madam Wu has taken you as one of her own, so that even I will have a difficult time convincing her. Especially after the near-tragedies you and the others have experienced. However, I will prevail. Count on it.

"Now don't do anything rash and everything will be all right."

Mei-hua and Guei-lung bowed low and left the office. Relief flooded through her. Once again the judge was coming to her rescue. She silently promised to be a paragon of virtue and female propriety—at least for the next couple of days.

Chapter 12

DOUBLE FIFTH DAY, as the holiday was known, began auspiciously. The sun peeked over the horizon, brightening a clear sky. Moist, warm soil released an earthy bouquet, which spoke of new growth. A parade of water buckets carried past their window sloshed rhythmically, reminding Mei-hua that she and Ping-an needed to prepare for the day's special herbal bath.

Pungent eupatorium herbs—with their acrid, aromatic qualities—had been gathered in the fall, sun-dried, and cut into pieces before storing. Today, the herbs would infuse bathwater for the family. While everyone would enjoy the bath, it was considered especially important for the daughters of the house. The eupatorium-imbued water prevented diseases, awoke the spleen, and ameliorated the season's dampness and heat. Mei-hua looked forward to savoring its qualities. She smiled, remembering that her father always kept this herbal bath tradition in their home as well.

When the water was warmed and ready, Ping-an and Mei-hua went to the bathing room together. Mei-hua removed the jade amulet her father had given her and placed it safely on a shelf. As the maids assisted them in preparing for their baths, Ping-an sang softly. The melodious notes soothed and calmed her. For, as much as Mei-hua looked forward to the warm, cleansing water, Ping-an feared the pain she would suffer as her bound feet were unwrapped to allow them to be properly cleaned.

Silent tears rolled down Ping-an's cheeks as Lotus Blossom gently removed the long strips of cloth which firmly tied her foot bones into their broken, distorted shape.

"Mistress, don't cry. You have beautiful feet. So tiny. Your future husband will be delighted to have such a wife," Lotus Blossom soothed.

But Mei-hua had to look away as the wraps revealed Ping-an's foot, with its toes tucked under her sole and its unnaturally high arch of broken bones. For hundreds of years, Han women sought lotus feet as a sign of great beauty. Their husbands never beheld the broken foot itself, only a wrapped foot encased in a splendid embroidered slipper.

Once the attendant had washed the tiny feet, however, and let them soak in the still lukewarm water, Ping-an relaxed.

"Are your feet better?" Mei-hua asked.

"Much. They only throb now. The sharp pain is gone."

"I'm glad. You're brave. I wouldn't be able to stand the pain," Mei-hua said.

Ping-an looked over at her in surprise.

"I mean it. When my aunt tried to bind my feet, I cried so much and so loud, my father finally gave in and told her to not do it. Although I was quite small, I remember how angry she had been. She told him that no one would want to marry me because I would have such big feet." Warmth spread up from her chest, over her neck, and into her cheeks. Talking about her feet always made her uncomfortable and embarrassed. Despite her happiness with not having broken bones, she knew what most of the people around her thought about the size of her feet.

"You may think I'm brave, but as a child, I really had no choice. It was my parents' decision. They did what was best for me." Nevertheless, a look of pride crossed Ping-an's face.

After their baths, as Lotus Blossom again tightly wrapped Ping-an's feet in fresh bandages, Mei-hua noticed her friend tried hard not to cry at the renewed pain. Ping-an didn't wear the seasonal mugwort or calamus sandal. Instead, her maid slipped on a pair of brightly colored shoes with a tiger embroidered on each one. Her gossamer silk skirt and blouse were the colors of summer—various shades of green—with bamboo and flower designs woven into the fabric. Bright and finely embroidered images of the five poisonous animals covered her overcoat. Mei-hua wore a similar coat over a silk blouse and matching flowing pants of a brilliant, multi-hued blue. She wore a pair of mugwort slippers Madam Wu had given her.

The maids did the girls' tresses in the same style—the Han-inspired fashion that had become so popular since the beginning of the Ming Dynasty eight years ago. A long braided ribbon of five-colored silk decorated their hair. As a last touch, the maids carefully embedded a carved hairpin of calamus root into one of the tightly knotted buns on either side of their heads. Ping-an's hairpin was of a frog and Mei-hua's of a tiger. As with all of their other garments today, they warded off the five evils and assured the wearer they would have health and peace.

When they had finished dressing, the two girls examined each other's appearance. They looked so similar, they really could have been cousins. They giggled in delight and hugged.

"What a day this will be!" Ping-an chortled. "And we are ready for it." With that, she twirled around, causing her skirt to float up in a circle. Lotus Blossom jumped to her side to keep her from tipping over. Ping-an gleefully sang out a few lines of her favorite popular song as she grabbed hold of her maid's arm, steadying herself once more.

Orchid stepped into the room. "Madam said you should rest and then we will leave for your Aunt Xi's. She'll let you know when the carriages arrive."

Back in their rooms, Ping-an sat watching her song bird and Mei-hua read. It wasn't long before Madam Wu sent an attendant over again to tell them to come to the courtyard. The carriages were ready.

Since Judge Hsu was going with them, an impressive array of soldiers, flag bearers, and horse-drawn vehicles filled the courtyard. The ornately carved vehicles were large enough to hold four people at a time. Mei-hua, Ping-an, and Madam Wu entered one; their maids and attendants boarded the others. The judge and Guei-lung rode separately. A drummer marched at the front of the entourage, followed by a group of soldiers. Next, the official magistrate's flag bearer came—alerting people to the riders' importance—then the carriages, and finally another small grouping of soldiers. Mei-hua noted that there was no sign of Soldier Guo. Finally, the magistrate's family's procession slowly filed through the street to Aunt Xi's compound.

Mei-hua settled in next to Ping-an. The distance was short, but tradition required a high government official travel in splendor. Such a procession ensured his, and the government's, image of authority and guaranteed respect. As they moved through the crowded streets, the throngs of people stepped aside to let them pass.

Uncle Fei, Aunt Xi, Grandma Fei, and their cousins had gathered to greet them as they disembarked from the carriages. Enthusiastic and cheerful greetings were passed around as everyone prepared to celebrate Duanwu together.

They went into the main garden, which had been decorated in red pomegranate flowers, with similar mugwort and calamus figures to the ones Madam Wu had placed around their compound. At the entrance near a fish pond, hung the largest image Mei-hua had ever seen of the demon queller, Zhang Kuei. Uncle Fei proudly showed them the picture, which he had received from a local literati and poet. Zhang Kuei stepped firmly on a demon while, at the same time, releasing the bat and good fortune out into the family's home.

Further into the garden, long banquet tables had been placed among massive rocks and huge pots of flowering plants and trees. Floral scents mingled with the pungent aroma of foods being prepared in the kitchen. Behind the tables ran a set of tall folding screens decorated with gleaming white flowers set against a shimmering backdrop of gold and framed in black lacquered wood. Golden-green bamboo tops peeked over the screens, making the flowers appear a natural part of the garden.

Everyone sat around the tables, with honored guests—the oldest and most noteworthy men—at the head table with Uncle Fei. The women mostly clustered together around Grandma Fei and Aunt Xi. Grandma Fei wanted Ping-an to sit closer to her, but the girl politely declined, saying she didn't deserve such an honor. Her Grandmother let her go in the end, allowing Mei-hua and Ping-an to place themselves at the end of the women's table.

The women's table was a kaleidoscope of colors and brilliant silks embroidered with elaborate designs to ward off the five evils. Calamus root hairpins jostled against gold and silver hairpins displaying birds and flowers. They were a festive picture set against the more conservative and moderated one of the men, who wore mostly grey and dark-colored robes commensurate with their status and rank as scholars and officials.

Mei-hua quickly picked out Guei-lung sitting at a table with the men. He had been placed in a more central position that reflected his promise as a scholar and as a symbol of the Hsu family's future. She watched him, noticing how comfortably he took his place among the other men. He sat further up the table and had not demurred, as his sister had, to chose a lesser spot instead.

She was quickly distracted, however, by the elaborate plates of food the attendants started bringing out. There were many dishes that were only eaten on this special festival: *zongzi*, the pyramid-shaped dumplings of glutinous rice and meat wrapped in bamboo leaves and tied together with the five-colored threads. Of course, there were some zongzi made with lotus seed paste especially for Grandma Fei, who ate no meat. Zongzi were Mei-hua's favorite of the Double Fifth Day foods. A burst of joy filled her at the first bite into the sweet, sticky rice. This was only one of more than a dozen main dishes and many small dishes, each served separately to be savored on its own. Fish, shrimp, pork, eggs, vegetables, fried wheat, and rice pancakes: the list was long and tasty to the very last bite.

Much of the conversation revolved around this afternoon's dragon boat races, who had won last year, and who might win this year. Cities, towns, villages, and even a few grand families had boats entered in the race. Mei-hua thought about the dragon boat they had seen in the warehouse and wondered who owned it. Her mind started to wander, looking for connections between the tea-horse trade thieves and her father's predicament.

"And what about the archery contest? I understand the Emperor himself watches such contests in his capital," Mei-hua heard a loud voice from the men's table say.

"Ooh," Ping-an breathed. "That's supposed to be so exciting. But, of course, I've never seen it," she finished with a slight pout.

"I haven't either," Mei-hua said. "Since it's a contest for young men to demonstrate both their horsemanship and archery skills, I'm sure it's fun. I wonder if Guei-lung will enter."

Ping-an giggled. "You've seen him shoot. He'd never win and it'd be too embarrassing for him to lose." She glanced at her brother as he and the rest of the men's table toasted each other and downed a cup of wine. His face was beginning to turn a bright red. "He does ride well, though. He doesn't get out enough on the horses, but he tells me he's quite good."

"Hsu Dou-wu was excellent in the contest when he was a young man," Grandma Fei said.

"Please, Grandma Fei, tell us what he did so we can honor him," Ping-an said. Her mother smiled at her and nodded.

"It was many years ago, before he married. The men had to ride a galloping horse while shooting willow arrows. The main contest was to hit a gourd hanging on a willow tree. A pigeon was inside the gourd."

A stir of sympathy for the pigeon made Mei-hua look down at her plate.

"The idea was for the best archer to hit the gourd and thereby release the pigeon unharmed. Not an easy task, as you can imagine." She grinned at her audience. "But, our Judge Hsu Dou-wu did it. He rode furiously around the field, sped past the tree and let an arrow fly. To the crowd's delight, the gourd burst apart, freeing its prisoner. The roar from the audience could be heard all the way to the sacred mountain, Tai Shan."

The women clapped and cheered, startling the men who looked over at them in wonderment.

"Grandma Fei is telling the story of Hsu Dou-wu winning the archery competition," Madam Wu called over, pride evident in her voice.

"A lucky shot," he modestly replied as all of the other men at the table lent their voices in praising his win. It was a tale the men knew well.

Mei-hua noticed that Guei-lung raised his cup to toast him, but didn't look particularly comfortable.

"Guei-lung!" a robust voice called to him. "Will you enter the competition and uphold your family's reputation?"

Before Guei-lung could answer, his father broke in, "I was older than he is now. Perhaps in another couple of years. Right now he has been concentrating more on his books than on these other skills."

"Father really saved his face this time," Ping-an whispered into Mei-hua's ear and shook her head in sympathy for her brother.

"Ah, well," the raucous-voiced man said, "I understand that most of the competitors will be soldiers this year."

"Yes. One of the guards, a Soldier Guo, will be entering," Judge Hsu said.

Mei-hua lifted her head at this and Ping-an clapped her hands. Guei-lung looked a little ill, although Mei-hua thought that could be because he'd eaten too much.

"Isn't he related to Lord Chiu?" Auntie Xi asked.

Her brother-in-law looked over at her. "Yes. He's been with my office for the past several weeks."

"So, will he represent the court in the archery contest?"

"No, each contestant represents himself. They are not sponsored in the way the dragon boats are. The archery contests are for personal skills and abilities. In his case, however, Lord Chiu sent a request to allow him time off from his duties so he could participate in the contest."

Mei-hua listened carefully. So that was why she hadn't seen him today and the guards attending to her were unfamiliar. She had wondered if Soldier Guo's absence was due to the judge's belief he was a spy. Now it seemed the reason he wasn't here was because he was to be a contestant in the archery contest.

She nudged Ping-an. "Do you think there'd be some way we could see the archery contest and the dragon boat races? Guei-lung and the other boys will be going."

"There will be huge crowds," she frowned. "I don't think Father will allow it."

Mei-hua pursed her lips. "There's got to be a way."

"If there is, I'm sure you'll find it." Her comment made Mei-hua happy; whatever resentment Ping-an had expressed the other day seemed to have vanished.

Looking up at Grandma Fei, Mei-hua had an idea. "Honorable Ancestor," she said, "your story about Uncle Hsu and the archery contest was so stirring it makes me wish we ladies could see such a contest, too."

"It is a time when so many come to revel in the strengths of these young men," Grandma Fei said, "including many women. However, our position is more sensitive and it is not as easy for us."

"It would be wonderful to see the games, though," one of Ping-an's cousins chimed in. Several other women at the table nodded their heads or vocally added their support.

"We could take the carriages to a high spot and, while remaining inside, see the horses and the shooting," Mei-hua offered.

Several women enthusiastically agreed.

Grandma Fei smiled benignly over the group. Although strict with her own lifestyle, she was known to be permissive with her family and easily gave way to their pleading. "You youngsters are full of ideas. Such a plan would work well."

The table once more filled with rapid and excited chatter as everyone looked forward to their treat.

The leisurely dinner, which allowed everyone to luxuriate in witty company, lasted until mid-afternoon. Such a banquet was to be savored and enjoyed, not hurried through. Food was not only a goal in itself, but also a pretext to take pleasure in everyone's company. As Mei-hua sat back, she ruminated on the idea that eating slowly was the only way she could eat so much. She surreptitiously tapped her tummy in satisfaction. Finally, fruit was brought to the tables, signaling the last dish and the end of the dinner.

Judge Hsu, who had to return to court, had already retired from the extended family dinner. However, he left orders with Guei-lung to inform Mei-hua he wanted to discuss information he'd recently received from her father. While the judge didn't want to disturb his in-laws' special holiday celebration, he wanted Guei-lung to escort his cousin back to the compound as soon as it was polite for them to leave. Therefore, immediately after dinner, Mei-hua prepared to return to court. Ping-an and the rest of the household remained at the Xi compound, resting after the bountiful banquet.

Leaving Orchid behind and taking Lotus Blossom with her, Mei-hua entered the main courtyard. Their carriage would follow behind Guei-lung's carriage. However, before stepping into the enclosed space, Guei-lung came up to her, excitement clearly written on his face.

"Little cousin, I was at the entrance just now when I saw Soldier Guo."

"I would have thought he'd be preparing for the archery contest," Mei-hua said, "and taking care of his horse."

Guei-lung nodded vigorously, "And there's more."

She hated it when he dragged out what he wanted to say. "What? What else?"

"I saw him on the street across from our gate; he was with one of those ruffians we saw at the warehouse."

A shiver ran through Mei-hua. Soldier Guo is a part of the gang, but what's he doing here, across from the Xi compound? "Do you think he knows you recognized him?"

"Perhaps. When I approached the gate, he immediately turned away as if to hide his face. I'm sure he didn't want me to identify him. There's no doubt. As we thought, he's mixed up with the enemy."

Chapter 13

MEI-HUA COULDN'T SEE much through the main gates when she reached the carriage, although tantalizing street noises hinted at the heightened level of activity on the other side of their wall. Lively sounds of rumbling carts and hawkers enticing buyers with their high-pitched calls drew her attention. She paused halfway into the carriage and glanced out toward the streeet once more. An explosion of cymbals and the boom of drums announced the beginning of a puppet play. Startled by the sudden sounds, the carriage's horse whinnied and pulled it forward before Mei-hua had completely stepped into it. Momentarily thrown off balance, Lotus Blossom caught her as she stumbled backward.

"Hold that horse!" Guei-lung called to a soldier, who rushed forward and calmed it down. "This one's too spirited and high strung," the young man said to Mei-hua, a frown knitting his brow. He glanced over at his carriage. "Mine's older and more experienced, so the noises and crowds don't bother him. We should exchange your horse with mine."

"No, it's fine. The horse is quiet now; it's under control." Mei-hua said. Exchanging horses would take some time and she wanted to get back. She was anxious to hear the new information from her father.

Guei-lung shot her an aggravated glance, but nodded.

Soon they were on their way out of the main gates and into the raucous street. As had become her habit by now, Mei-hua carefully pushed the curtain aside to peer out. She looked for Soldier Guo. He was nowhere in sight. The crowd made it difficult to locate one person in such a massive gathering. Even sitting higher in the carriage didn't help. The crush of people produced a blur of humanity. Soldiers, merchants, shoppers, tourists, children, vendors, and impromptu actors and acrobats vied for the road's limited space.

The carriages laboriously moved through the throng. All around them, peddlers from the various food carts loudly enticed passersby to purchase their fresh Duanwu cakes and zongzi. Eyeing the carts, she was reminded of how much she had just enjoyed these tasty holiday specialties at the banquet. She had overheard the maids talking about the Duanwu festival and sharing memories of their favorite foods. Even the poorest family tried to splurge at this time of year and either buy or make the holiday delicacies. Mei-hua's favorite, zongzi, had turned out to be their favorite, too.

After passing one more food stand, she impulsively decided to stop and buy a few for the maids in the Hsu women's quarters. Not all of the maids and attendants were able to come with them to the party at Aunt Xi's home. After the dinner, the servants brought to attend the family at the party would have their own small feast. She thought of those left behind at the house who would not be able to enjoy any holiday specialties.

She saw a zongzi food cart up ahead and knocked on the carriage ceiling. "Stop! Stop!" She grinned at Lotus Blossom. "I'll get a few treats to take back."

Lotus Blossom's relaxed posture went rigid, announcing her discomfort at such a move. However, she merely said, "I'll go. How many do you want?"

Mei-hua scooted toward the door. "It's all right. I'll get them."

Apparently alarmed at her young mistress's impetuous move, Lotus Blossom tried to intercept her. She put a hand on Mei-hua's arm. "Really, Madam Wu would prefer that you didn't. I can do it. Or, if you would like, our escort could easily purchase whatever you need."

"That won't be necessary," Mei-hua laughed, pleased to be able to do something to brighten the holiday for the maids. "The stall is right here. Really, I'll be quick." She released Lotus Blossom's hand and stepped out of the carriage.

As her feet touched the ground, she instinctively reached for her jade amulet for reassurance that all was safe for her to venture out. Her fingers found nothing. Mei-hua remembered she'd taken the amulet off when she and Ping-an had their traditional herb baths this morning. She smiled. No problem. She'd retrieve it later when they returned home. What could go wrong now?

Her maid promptly followed. Mei-hua flashed her another smile of delight and continued into the street. Almost immediately, she was surprised at how hard she had to shove through the suffocating crowd.

The guard accompanying her carriage watched them, confusion written on his face. This was an unexpected development. Neither Mei-hua nor Guei-lung told him what to do, so he remained in his position behind her carriage. Lotus Blossom stayed glued to Mei-hua's side. She attempted to keep people at bay as her mistress pressed on toward the small cart which proffered piles of the sticky rice mixture, each morsel enshrouded in green leaves and tied closed with a piece of twine.

Before she reached the cart, Guei-lung appeared at her side.

"What are you doing?" he sputtered. "Mother will never forgive me for this. Can't you just do what's expected once in a while?"

She looked up into his furious eyes with as innocent an expression as she could muster. "I'm only trying to bring some pleasure into the lives of our maids," she said. "They work so hard and this will be an unexpected treat for them."

Guei-lung harrumphed, causing her to grin mischievously. "Come on, Guei-lung. We'll be quick. Besides, we're almost home. There's no problem."

"You know Mother will find out. You can't give the maids gifts and not expect her to hear of it. We'll both be in trouble. Again. Are you purposely trying to aggravate her? She's only trying to do what's best for you." As he said this, he pushed a man aside so she could move forward. The fellow cursed him and fell backward.

Having reached the food cart, Mei-hua used it as an excuse to not respond. She did chafe at the restrictions Madam Wu constantly placed, or at least tried to place, on her. So was he right? Was she just trying to aggravate her guardian? She shook her head. No. Not long ago, Mei-hua herself had been a maid in the Hsu-Wu household, and her memories of that experience gave her greater sympathy for the women who, unlike her, would spend their lives in service. Right now, she just wanted to buy a few zongzi for the maids in her household to enjoy. Was that too much to ask? Was that too complicated?

Mei-hua glanced at the other shoppers, mostly farmers and laborers or their wives. She stared at the few women around her. They wore neat, but simple, cotton skirts and blouses with their long jackets. A couple of young women had lovely flowers embroidered on their jackets' front panels. The embroidery thread was cotton, not silk. They all wore bracelets of the five-colored threads. One woman held a wriggling child with a tiger painted on its forehead to ward off evil.

A new feeling rose up in her. If these women could be out in public, she thought rebelliously, why not her? After all, she was only buying treats for the servants. It wasn't like she was out committing crimes and bringing dishonor on the family. She puffed her cheeks in self-righteous indignation.

"Young Lady, may I help you? My zongzi are the best. You'll not find any better on the street or in the whole of Hangzhou," the vendor said, interrupting her thoughts. He smiled at her, showing off a gaping mouth with three remaining teeth. "I have zongzi with pork, egg, or lotus seed paste. What is your choice?"

Mei-hua bought several of each. Wrapped in glistening bamboo leaves they all looked the same. The vendor wrote out the main ingredient in each bundle and tied them together, allowing her to tell each group apart from the other.

"Now are you ready to return?" Guei-lung grumbled.

She nodded and handed Lotus Blossom her purchases.

With Guei-lung leading the way, and her maid still glued to her side, Mei-hua turned and started back. A volley of curses erupted near her carriage. A group of men jostled about. Two yelled and tried to strike out at each other. They were each restrained by bystanders, some of whom held the would-be fighters apart, while others seemed to be taking sides. In a flash, a general fight had broken out.

Her guard tried to intervene, although the growing crowd of men easily outnumbered him. He yelled for them to disperse and struck several with his staff, all to no avail.

People fell back from the fighting core, escaping possible danger. This sudden surge caused the crowd to push even harder against Mei-hua, separating her from Guei-lung and Lotus Blossom.

She struggled to return to her carriage, but the mass of bodies pressing in the opposite direction was too thick to penetrate. A claustrophobic smell of body odor mixed with the high humidity made her nauseous. She tried to put a hand over her mouth and nose, but she couldn't even lift an arm in the oppressive crowd.

A calloused hand the size of a dinner plate closed over her mouth. An arm encircled her waist and pinned her arms against her sides. Mei-hua frantically searched for someone to notice. All eyes were on the chaos which had broken out near her carriage. She thrashed about, wrestling with her attacker; she tried to kick him, but she couldn't bring her knees up. The crowd had become a tightly bound blanket encasing her. Movement was impossible.

But not for her attacker.

Stapled against a brawny chest, the attacker dragged her sideways, away from the vendor's cart, her carriage, Guei-lung, and her guard—away, she desperately realized, from safety.

Chapter 14

HE CAN'T GET AWAY WITH THIS; there are too many people, Mei-hua thought, her eyes flashing around the area. She frantically hoped someone would notice.

No one paid any attention to the girl being dragged through the crowd.

Mei-hua and her attacker didn't go far. Within a few steps, he hustled her through a small doorway. The interior's darkness engulfed them, hiding them from prying eyes. Once inside, however, her legs were free from the crowd's constricting grip, and she began anew to kick and squirm.

She tried to free her arms. No luck. She couldn't break his iron hold. She tried to wrap her legs around his, to halt his walking. No luck.

"You wild brat. If you don't stop this, I'm going to have to get tough," he said in a raspy voice, giving her a sharp jerk. Her head snapped back. She winced.

As he dragged her into the building, her feet scrapped against the wood floor and one of her slippers caught on a rough board. Her captor didn't notice. He just kept pulling her deeper into the darkened room. Her mugwort slipper didn't give way and the board pulled it off her foot.

So much for averting evil, she thought in dismay. Despite her general skepticism toward good luck charms, she would have been happy if the mugwort had done its duty and protected her. Certainly this man was evil itself.

Realizing flailing around didn't help, she went limp and he nearly dropped her.

"Think you're clever, do you?" he said, quickly adjusting his hold. He clasped her so tightly she could barely breathe.

Her abductor carelessly knocked her against a doorway when he pulled her through it, causing a stab of pain to radiate from her elbow. She bit her lip to keep from crying out.

Although the blackness obliterated even the vaguest of shapes around them, a shuffling and slight thump alerted her to the presence of someone else in the room. At least, she hoped it was another person and not rats. Rats were worse than criminals. She figured she might be able to at least reason with criminals, but reasoning would never work with flesh eating rodents.

"I'm going to put you down. Behave and you won't get hurt." He took her to a chair and dropped her into it. "Now, I'm going to uncover your mouth; don't scream. It's useless anyway. Your screams mean nothing in this holiday crowd." He chuckled and began slowly removing his thick hand from her face. She remained silent.

He pulled his hand away. "Good. That's good." He started to straighten up and lean away from her.

Fresh air flooded back into her lungs and Mei-hua shrieked with all her might, "HEL ..."

An explosion of pain shot through her head, followed by total black.

*****

Her head throbbed with unrelenting misery. Nausea followed right behind. The torment caused by the slightest motion immediately forced her to cease all movement. She had to remain still.

"...it's almost time," a hoarse voice said.

"What will we do with her until then?" the familiar raspy voice asked.

"Keep her hidden, of course, you idiot."

"She's awfully aggressive and feisty."

"What? Are you afraid of a little girl?" the hoarse voice mocked.

"'Course not. But, I'm just saying, it might not be so easy."

The other man snickered. "Never thought I would see the day you worried about a girl."

A loud curse and the crash of ceramic bursting into bits startled Mei-hua. She jerked in an involuntary spasm.

"Ha! You woke our sleeping maiden," the hoarse voice said.

Mei-hua tried to quiet her breathing and appear unconscious.

A pressure on her shoulder hardened and shook her violently. The pain in her head magnified. She squeezed her eyes tightly closed, trying to shut out the pain.

"Do. Not. Play games. With me."

The hand jerked her shoulder again, even harder.

Bile rose in Mei-hua's throat. She wanted to vomit. She wanted to stop the knives slicing her fragile brain. She wanted to end the torment.

Cautiously, in spite of piercing, stabbing, pain, she managed to open her eyes. It was as if she peered through a gauze curtain—and the view was not auspicious.

She recognized the evil-faced man sitting on a stool opposite her. Ching Da. A muscle-bound ruffian stood glowering behind him.

She closed her eyes again. Was this a bad dream? As much as she wished it, she knew the answer was no. The pain was too real. She'd never had a dream like this before. It would be impossible.

She opened her eyes a little wider. Now the gauze curtain had almost dissolved. The men and the room were becoming disconcertingly clear.

"That's better," Ching Da said. He grinned, then asked with a sneer, "Are you wondering how you ended up here? The answer is easy: masterful planning. We watched you constantly," he bragged, snorted loudly, and added, "and, of course, fate. It was fate that caused you to leave your carriage in the middle of that teeming street. You couldn't have played into our hands any better if we had paid you." His laughter turned into another jarring snort.

Mei-hua stared at him, eyes half shut. Even with the shooting pain almost incapacitating her, she realized she had gotten herself into a serious problem.

"You're safe. You're in my protective arms," he mocked and held his arms wide. The man behind him broke into a horselaugh, spewing saliva in a spray.

Ching Da wiped his sleeve and punched the fellow. "Spit in a different direction, you fool!"

The man wiped his mouth, but continued to laugh.

Throughout this exchange, Mei-hua glanced around the room and down at her arms tied to a chair. Instead of the fine silk clothing she'd had on when she left for the visit to the Xi household, she now saw a coarse, white cloth covering her arms. She stole a look at her lap and saw that the rest of her clothing had also been replaced with the same undyed, rough cotton.

She trembled. Had they disrobed her to put on these new clothes? Fear played in the back of her mind. What happened while she was unconscious?

"Did you think you could hide, pretending to be a relative of the Hsu's?" he taunted.

She listened with one ear, but continued to inspect her clothing. Could it give her a clue as to what happened? This jacket was a mourning coat. When a close relative died, people wore special mourning clothing made of simple, uncomfortable cotton cloth for many, many months. Why was she wearing this? In the veil of confusion caused by the throbbing in her head, she found it impossible to focus.

Did someone die? Her father? She looked at the cloth again. Yes, it was what an unwed daughter would wear when her father died. A wash of depression began to mingle with her head's unrelenting throbbing.

She choked back a sob. Her father had died.

Still blurry-eyed and unable to concentrate through the pain, she watched Ching Da. Did he kill her father? Anger began to replace the depression and even overtake the pain.

"We are not so simple. You people in high society think we commoners are too stupid to know what is happening. We know. We all know more than you think."

She wondered at his bizarre monologue. Nevertheless, she started paying attention. Now she knew for sure who was after her family. But she also needed to learn why she and her father had become targets. And, just as importantly, she needed to find their weaknesses. She had to escape, not only to save herself, but to avenge her father.

"Of course," he snickered, his face thrust close to hers, "it helps to have friends in high places."

Mei-hua froze. Lord Chiu and his adopted son, Soldier Guo. She fumed. She may be as insignificant as a mustard seed, but she would not let this travesty go unpunished!

"The afternoon will be over soon," the other fellow said.

Ching Da nodded. "We'll talk again," he said to Mei-hua and stood up. "Put her in the box."

The burly fellow came around and began untying Mei-hua, careful to keep his body pushed tightly against her so that she couldn't jump out of the chair and escape. He didn't bother to wait for her to stand; he grabbed her waist, hoisted her over his shoulder, and carried her across the room.

She wanted to fight against him, but the pain and nausea were still too strong. She was incapable of struggling, so she continued to use all of her remaining strength to focus on the men and what they said. Their conversation would give her the clues she needed.

A large wooden box with loosely joined slats stood by the warehouse door. As the fellow reached it, he hoisted her higher up onto his shoulder and pulled the door open. Shifting his weight, he shoved her inside.

She landed against the wooden floor. A splinter rammed into the palm of her hand; she winced and sucked at the new wound. Mei-hua crouched against the side of the cage, arms over her head. A tug-of-war between depression and a furious anger, tinged with desire for revenge, waged inside her.

The door shut and she heard metal slide against metal. They'd locked the box's door. Without another word, the two men left. As their footsteps grew dimmer, she pushed herself up into a sitting position against the rough-cut wooden slats.

For a while, all she could hear was a *shiiir, shiiir, shiiir*. She crawled to the front of the cage and squinted through the space between the slats. The sound came from large containers being slipped across the floor. Lines of men shoved containers and carried large bundles out of the warehouse. She moved crab-like along her prison's side, searching for a larger gap to peer through. Finally, she was able to peer out of a wider opening. The burly man was sitting on a stool not far from her. Beyond him, men moved bales and crates across the warehouse floor and out the door.

She suddenly knew where she was. This was the warehouse she and Guei-lung had spied on earlier. The one with the tea and brocades meant for the Imperial government's tea-horse trade.

After a short time, the repetitive nature of the men's activities relaxed her. The intermittent shouting back and forth had only to do with the movement of bales and boxes, nothing related to her and her predicament. Men putting the finishing touches on the dragon boat moved over the wooden beast in studied concentration. They were nearing the end of their work. It was almost time to enter the race.

She sat slumped against the boards and kept a casual eye on the warehouse activities, waiting for something to happen. Her mind began to wander. Her eyes glazed over as she willed the pain away and ruminated about her predicament.

She started to fall asleep when she became aware of a change. It was the silence in the vast room that caught her attention.

She peered through the space between the box's slats. An entourage had started moving through the main warehouse opening. Someone cried, "*Gu long lai*! Look around, the dragon comes."

In the middle of the cluster of entering men strode a pear-shaped man in a long, dark robe. He swung his feet along as if kissing the ground, hands behind his back. He stopped to inspect the dragon boat as the men began to move it out of the warehouse and onto the wharf.

There was no mistaking him for anything other than the boss and—she guessed by the long dark robe and soft black cap he wore—probably a local elite who ran the important civil affairs in his town, city, or even district. But, Mei-hua wondered, where was he from? Hangzhou? She scrutinized him closely.

She slowed her breathing so that its delicate sound didn't interfere with her hearing every word—even if spoken quietly or in a hushed voice.

She didn't have to worry. The boss's voice boomed throughout the warehouse.

"Ching Da! Why are you so far behind? We must move more quickly. The dragon boat race begins shortly. What are you doing?"

Ching Da came forward and, with a curt bow, said, "Greetings, Boss. The loading is going smoothly." He paused. "And the other shipment you wanted is here, as requested."

"Where is she?" the portly fellow demanded.

Ching Da grinned. "Follow me."

They started toward the box. Unconsciously, Mei-hua shrank back before she realized they couldn't see her. Returning to her former position, she pressed against the slats, looking through the narrow space between them once more. She would memorize the boss's features and remember him always.

As they crossed the floor toward her holding cell, she heard him say, "Judge Zhang thinks he can break me." He laughed, but there was little mirth in it. "This'll show him what happens to those not wise enough to go along with me."

Mei-hua sunk down. *What did this mean? Was her father alive? Alive, but still in danger?* She looked down at her mourning clothing. It didn't make sense.

Chapter 15

MEI-HUA QUIETLY PUSHED HERSELF into the back corner of the cage, as far from the door as she could get. As she moved backward, her mourning jacket fell open at her knees. A sapphire blue shimmered in the dim bar of light streaming in from the openings between the cage's slats. She caught her breadth.

Leaning forward, she gently pulled the white cotton jacket back even more. A scorpion appeared.

She smiled and quickly pushed the rough over-gown off her knee. The five evil animals danced across her long, silk vest. She ran a finger over each one and her smile grew.

The mourning jacket covered the clothing she wore for Auntie Xi's Duanwu dinner. Nothing had happened to her father. Ching Da or his thug must have slipped the plain robe over her striking party dress. It occurred to her that they must have had to use the mourning jacket to hide her clothing as they moved her through the streets. People might remember a wealthy young woman dressed in elegant silk being carried unconscious through the city; however, they wouldn't think twice about it if the girl was in mourning. She could have fainted or been sick due to the distress of grief.

While happily examining her clothing, Mei-hua did not hear the men reach her prison-for-one.

"Open it!" Ching Da ordered.

She straightened, prepared for the intrusion. Metal jingled against metal, screeched, and, finally, clanked. The lock had given way and opened. Hinges squealed in protest as the door swung wide. A gloomy light suffused the box, replacing its dimly-striped darkness. She pulled the mourning jacket over her knees and remained pressed against the back wall.

"Get over here," Ching Da ordered. "I don't want to have to drag you out."

Mei-hua didn't respond. Stillness answered him. She knew he held all the pieces in this game, but she wasn't going to make it easy for him.

"Stop playing with her, idiot," the boss said, "I don't have all day."

"Get her," Ching Da growled.

A burly thug Mei-hua recognized as her kidnapper darkened the doorway and leaned into the box. Reaching over, he grabbed her wrists in a vise-like grip. She fell forward onto her chest as he began hauling her out. The boards tugged on her jacket as she scraped across them. He yanked her out of the box and left her lying on the dirt-encrusted warehouse floor. She kept her eyes down on the boots of the men around her.

"So this is Zhang Mei-hua," the boss said. He pushed his boot against her shoulder to make her turn over. She resisted and remained as she was. He removed his foot and said, "She doesn't look like much, but she'll be useful to us in the end."

"She's a handful; she'll be a lot of bother," Ching Da said.

"Bah. What's your problem? Can't you handle a girl? If I'd known you were such a wimp, I'd never have taken you and your gang on."

If she hadn't been in such misery and pain, Mei-hua would have laughed. This was almost exactly what Ching Da had said to his own lackey. *They have no imagination*, she thought disparagingly.

"There's no need to be insulting," Ching Da grumbled. "I can take care of her."

"Good. I'm expecting you to. We must not fail. We are ready for the big move and there's no room for mistakes."

"What do you want me to do?"

"Put her back in the box. We'll tend to her later."

"You heard him," Ching Da said. "Throw her back in the cage and be sure to lock it."

Once more the meaty hands reached for her, but Mei-hua quickly jerked to the side and scooted back into the cage.

The boss let out a loud guffaw. "Good move. Stay in the box and you'll be safe."

Ching Da joined him in a raucous jeer. As his thug closed and locked the door, Ching Da asked, "How long will we keep her? You know the Dragon Races will start shortly and after that my men will start transporting the goods."

"You don't need to remind me." The boss growled. "I know the schedule. I set it. We won't keep her long. That won't be necessary." Throwing his head back, he laughed, then stopped abruptly.

Nervous, Mei-hua quietly huddled against the cage's wall once more, peering through the slats and listening intently.

"Then what? She's seen us and can identify who we are; we could be arrested," Ching Da said.

"You worry too much."

"Easy for you to say, but I think this local magistrate, Hsu, is on to me and my men. I've received word that he's watching us. We have to be careful. I'm glad we're going to move this stuff out today."

"You don't have to worry about the law," the boss sneered. "That's why you're not the boss. You're too timid. To be the boss you have to know your enemy's weak points and not be afraid to put pressure on them."

"So, you're going to convince Judge Zhang to be on our side and give him back his girl?" Ching Da said.

"You're right on the first part and wrong on the second," the boss said, looking over at the men repacking tea into large, unmarked bales. He grinned and nodded in their direction. "Once we have our shipments safely installed in our own storage areas in Changsha, and ready for distribution, we'll package up our little morsel here—along with a few rocks—and drop her in the bay. A deluxe *zongzi* for the River Dragon!" He broke into a fit of laughter, choked, recovered, and walked back out toward the warehouse door.

Chapter 16

CHING DA SCURRIED AFTER HIM. The rest of their conversation was lost in the muddle of warehouse noises.

Mei-hua remained squinting through the slats. Ching Da's henchman sat at the front of her prison. He chewed on his nails, biting off pieces and spitting them out onto the floor. He looked like he wasn't going anywhere soon.

Moving as quietly as possible so as not to alert the guard, she carefully pushed and tugged on every slat, testing their strength, hoping to find one loose. After circling the entire cage, all she discovered was that her prison was strong, too strong for her to simply remove a board without tools.

She again peered out at her prison guard. His attention had turned to the warehouse workers. They appeared to be putting aside their tools. While he was distracted, she slipped her fingers between the door's slats and felt the lock. It was a sliding bolt, as she thought. Sighing in relief that it wasn't an iron padlock, she pushed hard against its end. It moved, but just barely.

The guard shuffled around, changing his position and stretching his shoulders. Mei-hua immediately withdrew. He shot a quick glance in her direction and then resumed watching the workers. One of them called over to him in a language Mei-hua didn't understand. The guard answered with a wordless frown. The other fellow started yelling out to him again, when Ching Da cut in sharply in the same unintelligible language.

The guard responded in a defensive tone, but settled back. He turned toward Mei-hua's box with an exasperated sigh and stared at it, scratching his armpit.

Although Mei-hua didn't understand what the men said, she was pretty sure it was the same dialect the locals spoke around Changsha where her father was magistrate. That meant the men were probably from the western region and not Hangzhou. They must have been brought in to do this job.

She wondered if the fat boss came from Changsha too. Probably. Otherwise, why would he use men from that area? If the boss was from there, it would go some way toward explaining why she had been kidnapped. Clearly, this man knew her father was a magistrate, was threatened by him, and wanted to use her to control him.

She looked past the guard and watched Ching Da. If the men in his gang were from her father's district, it suggested that at least the gang's home base was Changsha, not Hangzhou. Therefore, Changsha was a critical location for the crime they were planning to commit.

She thought about Soldier Guo. She couldn't remember why, but she was sure his family, or at least a branch of his family, was from Hangzhou City, not Changsha. She rubbed her head. Was that right?

And what about Lord Chiu? He certainly appeared to be the mastermind behind all this. With his high position in the Imperial government, he ultimately determined which merchants could get licenses to participate in the tea-horse trade.

And she couldn't believe it was a coincidence that the older brother of Changsha's Gate's owner was a government official in the tea-horse trade under Lord Chiu. She pressed her hands tightly against her head to give her relief from its non-stop pounding.

With the pain in her skull dampened but far from gone, she struggled to continue with her analysis. Perhaps the older brother was just one rung in the criminal ladder leading to Lord Chiu. He must have given the official government license to the boss. Otherwise, how else would the boss have the right to sell the tea and brocades for horses? She remembered the merchant bragging about having "friends in high places."

She shuddered at the thought that Lord Chiu was behind this whole mess. Yet, who else would have a spy network that worked so efficiently that it discovered where she was hidden? She, who was the weak link in her father's armor.

Mei-hua hung her head, supporting her chin with her hand. She was so tired. As she allowed herself to relax on the nest her hand created, the mugwort decorated hairpin slipped out of her hair. It clattered onto the crate's jagged floorboards. The hairpin's smooth, glistening surface contrasted with the pine's irregular grain. She picked it up and twirled it through her fingers. Grasping both ends, she pushed hard, trying to bend it. There was little give. She grinned and put the mugwort hairpin back into the once perfect, and now loosely dangling, knot in her hair. Perhaps this would be her good luck piece and would save her from evil after all.

Boots on the hard-packed dirt of the warehouse floor clomped toward her cage. She squinted through a break in the slats. Ching Da was coming. Behind him, two other men carried a small stool, package, and a folding table and chair, which they set up in front of her cage.

"Open the box," he ordered.

Once more, the door squeaked on opening and a gray light crowded into her claustrophobic prison.

"Now, little sister," he said, using a common term for a girl younger than the speaker, "we need to talk."

Mei-hua glared at him, but he just laughed.

"You've got spirit. I like that." He pursed his lips and shook his head. "Not that it will do you much good."

As he spoke, she noticed one of his men had already opened the table and placed the stool in front of it. Now he was preparing ink on the plain ink stone he'd pulled out of the package and had placed on the table near a sheet of rice paper.

"First, come out of there." He walked over to the military-style folding chair that had been placed on one side of the table.

She didn't move.

"Don't make this harder than it needs to be. It's been a long day and I don't have much patience for your foolishness." He rubbed a hand over his chin.

Mindful of his lackey dragging her out earlier, Mei-hua scooted toward the door; she couldn't stand up in the cage. Grabbing the side of the box's opening, she swung herself up and out. She stood before him, scowling. She was still somewhat muddled from the pain, but she wasn't going to give him the satisfaction of knowing how terrible she felt.

"Sit down, sit down," he said pointing to the stool. "You have a job to do."

She sat and wrapped the mourning robe over her lustrous pants and long vest.

"That's better." He leaned back into his folding chair. With his elbows resting on its arms, he pressed his fingers together to form a temple's roofline. He tapped the tips of his fingers thoughtfully against his chin.

"Your father," he began, "has been a very, very bad magistrate. He has forgotten the number one rule every magistrate should remember: don't mess with the local leaders and your betters. If you do, disaster will befall you and your family."

Mei-hua bristled at his comments but held her tongue. Her father was the magistrate; he would uphold the law no matter who was involved. He had the highest of ethical standards and, when pursuing justice, wouldn't be deterred by political pressures. She was sure of it.

"You see, he has gotten himself involved in a small case of thievery, a case he should have never concerned himself with," Ching Da continued.

"A case involving one of the local elite," she said.

"Ah, you are insightful for one so young," he grinned, showing teeth stained red with betel nut juice, a drug that made the chewer feel good and full of energy.

"My father is the Honorable Emperor's honest and righteous servant. In the end, everyone will know that," she said. She couldn't keep the anger out of her voice.

He shook his head. "You're so innocent, so young." He tapped the table. "Keeping good relations and being mindful of who is really important in a town is critical to a magistrate's well-being. Your father, on the other hand, seems to think he must follow the letter of the law. Bah. The law is flexible. It has to be." He smirked. "This is a lesson he'll soon learn."

"You're the people trying to destroy him, to poison him against the Emperor," she fairly spit out.

He nodded. "Tried to anyway. That route is taking too long. It turns out your father might prosecute the case and start arresting people before we can complete that scenario."

Mei-hua felt a flood of relief. They didn't think they could destroy him by making the Emperor believe he was a traitor. He was safe.

"So, now we have an alternate plan," he paused, staring at her. He pushed the sheet of paper closer to her on the table, took up the brush, and dipped it into the prepared ink. "You're going to write a note to your father."

She unconsciously slipped her hands into the sleeves of her blouse and straightened her back even more as she sat on the stool. He wasn't going to force her to do anything. She turned a defiant face toward Ching Da.

He guffawed. "You don't have a choice. I'm telling you, not asking you." He thrust the brush out toward her. "Take this if you value your life."

She remained still, unrelenting.

He leaned toward her and snarled, "Or, your father's life."

Chapter 17

HER HEAD DROPPED. She was unsure of everything except the pain in her head and body. Just as she thought her father was safe, this happens. She shook her head, confused. There was no way for her to know what was real and what was false. Finally, she looked at the paper and took the brush. Then, she glanced at him, waiting. The anger in her chest burned; she wanted to scrub that smirk off his face.

"Good. Write:

Father, I am fine. Please help my protectors to resolve Their small problem. They will keep me safe until you do."

She quickly wrote out the words as he dictated them to her.

"Now sign it, *your most dutiful daughter, Mei-hua.*"

After she signed it, he took the paper and read it over. "Not bad."

"He won't let you get away with your crimes," she said. She wanted to believe in her father's honesty and invincibility, but couldn't get rid of the nagging behind her brave thoughts. Would he value justice over her life and perhaps his own? Did she really want him to place a crime against the state at a higher level than their own survival?

But then she remembered the boss's parting words about wrapping her up into a bundle and dropping her in the river. Unless something miraculous happened, she wouldn't be seeing her father again, no matter what he did to protect her.

Ching Da rolled the paper up and slipped it into his sleeve.

"I was an idealist like you when I was young," he said.

His words startled her. She never thought of him as ever being young and certainly not an idealist. How dare he compare himself with her?

"I fought for our dynasty's founder. We fought in Mongolia, in southern China, everywhere. I wanted a new Han dynasty—everyone did. But, what have we got? Nothing is better for us, the common people.

"The Emperor is only concerned with consolidating power and destroying any possible resistance. That did not save my wife and child, who starved to death. While he worries only about his power, the people continue to suffer. I am through with suffering. We know that 'Heaven is high and the Emperor is far away.'" He smirked and tapped his stomach.

"While the Emperor is involved in his world, he has little influence over local affairs. So I am using the *local* power system, which has been in place for generations before this dynasty was born and will be in place for generations after this dynasty has disappeared. Your father needs to distinguish between what's serious and what's trivial."

"You think stealing from the Emperor is trivial?" she said.

He looked at her through narrowed eyes. "You know more than what's good for you." He rose abruptly. "Put her back." He turned and strode away.

His henchman sprang up from his squatting position. The stocky man looked down at her. Did she see sympathy in his eyes? He pressed his lips together, exhaled loudly, and waved his hand toward the box.

She stood up and slowly stepped back into her cage. The sound of wood closing on wood and the bolt slipping into place followed her. The dreary colorless interior turned back into a slate black and gray. With the door shut and locked, Mei-hua folded herself into a sitting position and leaned against the wall.

Now that the boss and Ching Da had gone, a few of the workers came to chat with her guard. She watched them between the slat's opening. Most of them spoke in another Chinese language, so their conversation was lost on her. However, one of the fellows spoke Mandarin, which the guard could also speak. At least, she was able to understand them.

"Which boat are you betting on?" the newcomer asked Mei-hua's guard.

"Ours, of course!" He spread his legs and slapped his knee. "Have you ever seen a finer dragon?"

"We've all bet on it, but I hear the dragon boat from Shanghai is fast and their team powerful. So strong they can paddle up-stream in a raging storm."

"You're a traitor! No one can beat our boat!" the guard steamed.

"Don't be angry. We all agree." He turned to look at the exit. "We have to leave, the races are starting soon. What about you?" He glanced at Mei-hua's box. "Can you come?"

"No. I'm on duty. I have to stay and guard our little beauty. All I will hear is the yelling and cheering."

"I don't know why you have to guard that thing. She can't get out. Why don't you come?"

Mei-hua's heart jumped. Would he leave?

"No. You know Ching Da would kill me if I left my post. Come back later and tell me how much we've won," he said with a grin.

She grimaced. Even thieves were loyal to their jobs. Too bad.

After the workers left, however, the hoots and hollers of the crowd became ever louder. Her guard stood, stretched, and started to gradually wander closer and closer to the warehouse door. Eventually, he slipped so far away she could no longer see him. She checked around the space she could see from her box. He wasn't there. She was sure he'd been unable to resist the excitement just outside on the river running past the warehouse and had gone to enjoy a look at the dragon boat races.

Mei-hua pulled out her mugwort hairpin and gingerly pushed it though the space between the door slats near the bolt. She tentatively held the hairpin with her left hand while she slipped the fingers of her right hand through another, more slender, space to control its movement. More by feel than sight, she transferred the needle from her left to right hand and lined it up with the bolt. She began to push. Nothing.

She stopped. Was it in the right place? She moved the needle's point around and felt the circle created by the bolt. This was right. She centered it on the bolt and pushed as hard and with as much consistency as she could.

A small movement rewarded her efforts. She shoved some more and then some more. The bolt moved with fits and starts. A newish lock, it wasn't smooth with age and use. Finally, the lock popped open.

She pulled the needle back and pressed against the door. With a creak, the door began to give way. She grabbed it, preventing it from swinging wide.

Once more, she peered between the slats. No one. Was her guard still entranced by the dragon boat races?

Remembering the slight squeak of the door, Mei-hua pushed against it with as much caution as possible.

Another creak stopped her. She held her breadth and squinted in the direction her guard had disappeared. But there was no one and no sound except for the excited crowds outside the warehouse. She cautiously pressed against the door once more. Another half-of-a-hand opening. Another creak. Another pause. Another push. Finally she had enough space to squeeze through.

Half crawling and then half standing, she propelled forward. Once out, she stood and began to step away when she realized she only wore one sandal. She'd lost the first when her abductor dragged her into hiding. Kicking the second mugwort sandal off her foot, she planted her bare feet shoulder width apart and stretched. Her tense muscles complained after being inside such a small space for so long. She had to carefully extend each muscle allowing them to discharge their stiffness.

She cast a sidelong glance at the mounds of tea bales and quickly stepped behind one of them. Peering around the bales, she took in the entirety of the warehouse. As expected, everyone had gone. They'd left for the Dragon Race, to see if they'd won their bets. She looked toward the oversized door at the back where the bales were loaded onto boats. She didn't see her guard. She hoped he'd stepped outside for a better view of the race. She looked over to the front door. No one.

With sure, rapid steps she made her way over to the entrance. Exhilarated at being so close to escaping, in the final few steps she dashed for the door. She threw it open and ran out—straight into the arms of Ching Da.

Chapter 18

MEI-HUA SPRANG BACK as Ching Da's arms shot out to enclose her. She dropped down and spun out to the left through the remains of tea and rice debris. The fine dust danced up and around her, stinging her eyes. She blinked rapidly to clear her vision. As she did, Ching Da's arms brushed the top of her head, closing on air. She jumped up and raced down the wharf towards the crowds watching the dragon boat races.

The rhythmic sound of running boots behind her pushed her forward. She was sure it was Ching Da, but she dared not slow down to look. Instead she kept her eyes focused on her objective: to reach the section of the wharf that was open to the public. With the races going on, she expected to find an enormous, tightly packed crowd of on-lookers. If she could get to them, she could disappear in the throng.

But only if she could reach them before Ching Da overtook her.

She saw the crowd immediately ahead. In the midst of the catcalls, hoots, and bellows encouraging the racers, she heard a voice behind her call her name. She smirked. Did Ching Da seriously think she would stop and chat?

In the flash of a bat's wing, she ran straight into the crowd and merged with the on-lookers. By keeping low as she pushed and struggled against the spectators, she managed to put a barrier of several layers of bodies between her and Ching Da.

Her sense of success was short lived, however. While the press of spectators protected her, providing a shield, they also kept her from being able to see where she should go. She fought down a rising sense of panic. What was the best route of escape? She didn't know. All she knew right then was that she had to get away from the wharf.

She paused momentarily, glanced around at the crowd, and plunged ahead once more. She was able to squeeze through her human shield by keeping low—not hard to do since the cheering men were so much taller than she was. She consistently pushed against the mass of humanity as it leaned toward the river. She struggled to go in the opposite direction from where they were looking.

She knew these men were all standing between the river and a wall of warehouses, which lined the wharf. If she headed away from the men and toward the area behind them, she'd eventually arrive at the warehouses and, hopefully, find an alley out of here.

She wrestled forward, keeping her head down and pulling her mourning gown more snuggly around her. Although she feared someone in his enthusiasm for the races might accidentally smash her unprotected, bare toes, she kept pushing through the tightly packed spectators.

Finally, there was a break in the crowd. She looked up. The entrance to an alley greeted her hungry eyes. She didn't know exactly where it went, but it obviously led away from the wharf and into the city. That was all she needed to know.

Before breaking out of her protective human shield, she paused and quickly looked around to see if Ching Da was in sight. No. She dashed for the narrow alleyway and its concealing deep shadows.

Once within its bosom, she stopped, leaned against a cool wall, and gasped for breadth. A few men shouldering bamboo poles with heavy baskets hanging on either end drifted through the narrow passageway. They were either laborers or small-scale peddlers more interested in making a few coppers than in the race. They ignored the young woman in mourning as she passed through the alley. She was not a good candidate for buying their wares.

Yips and yells from the riverfront reverberated through the passageway. Mei-hua put her hands over her ears and continued to try to steady her breathing. Even in the alley, her ears hurt with all the noise. She shut her eyes for a brief moment, then immediately opened them again.

She knew she couldn't stop. He'd find her. All he had to do was look for a likely alley leading away from the river. He might go to the wrong one, but he might not. She couldn't take the risk.

After taking a few more deep breaths, she adjusted her mourning jacket, retied her rope belt, and went on. She kept close to the wall, walking as swiftly as possible, while keeping pace with the others in the alley. She didn't want to draw attention to herself, to appear suspicious by running. Young women didn't do that. Especially those in mourning.

As a precaution, Mei-hua periodically peeked behind her to check if anyone was following. Everything appeared normal. She moved along. At the end of the alley, she met another street. This one over-flowed with people and the holiday spirit. The ubiquitous food vendors and herbalists called out to passersby to buy their delicacies or herbs.

Standing at the end of the alley, Mei-hua stared briefly at the mounds of herbs and herbal amulets with their promise of ensuring safety from evil. She wished it was so easy to be rid of the wicked and their hateful crimes and corruption. She glanced away; life was more complicated.

No matter. She pulled her shoulders down and straightened her back. She admonished herself: *don't stand here all day moping. Get going.* She moved out into the busy street, always trying to appear as if she really was a young woman in mourning. No one would expect her to be watching the races. Such behavior would be too inappropriate and unfilial for a young woman alone. She walked with deliberate steps—modest, yet decisive—as if she had an errand and was carrying it out.

Shortly, she came to another good sized street. Should she take it? She tried to remember how they had previously returned home from the warehouse. She had allowed herself to be distracted last time. There had been so many vendors; the street was filled with peddlers and merchants of various sized businesses. Now, gazing around, she became confused.

She stopped at a nearby stall and pretended to examine a religious talisman while she thought about the route she needed to take. Looking up at the street corner, she recognized a placard over a shop to the right; its name was painted in large, black characters. Yes, they had passed this store.

She plunged ahead, all the while checking to see if Ching Da had followed. So far she was safe, but he could come around a corner at any time. He wasn't stupid. It wouldn't take him long to figure out she had gotten away from the wharf and was trying to go back home. Her job, she told herself, was to get home without him finding her first.

The further she walked, the more confident she became. This was definitely the route they had taken before. In spite of the increased number of impromptu carts and puppet theaters vying for every parcel of space, she recognized more and more of the buildings and stores around her. She would be safe at home soon. One more turn and then only two more blocks.

It was all she could do to keep from running. She walked as quickly as she could to the last corner, to the last couple of blocks to safety. Gongs from the nearby theater rang out, announcing the beginning of a play. Children squealed in expectation. The gongs' clanging reverberated at a deafening level, their sound vibrating through her.

She hurriedly turned the corner and froze.

Soldier Guo stood in the middle of the intersection at the end of the block. He was monitoring all roads to the Hsu compound from that one spot.

She instantly stepped into a doorway and out of sight. How was she going to get past him and safely home?

Chapter 19

A CART OVERFLOWING with red and orange clothing embroidered with the five evil animals rolled toward the yamen. As it passed the doorway, Mei-hua stepped out and, using the cart as a buffer, moved back into the street she had just come from. She intended to walk up another block, to go around the compound. This route would take her to the servants' gate in the back where she could enter unnoticed.

Crossing the intersection, she kept her head slightly turned in the opposite direction—in case Soldier Guo saw her from his post. With her face hidden and wearing a coarse, white, mourning robe, she was sure he wouldn't recognize her.

Reaching the protection of the building on the other side of the intersection, Mei-hua wanted to peek down the road to see if Guo was still there, but didn't dare. She walked on with the same purposeful steps as before.

The little theater's gong started up again with a frantic beat, a beat that matched the throbbing of her heart. She was so close to safety. What bad luck to have successfully avoided Ching Da just to run into Soldier Guo. Then, another unwelcome thought crossed her mind: had Ching Da sent some of his men to follow her, too?

She began searching the crowd for familiar faces. Faces of the men she had seen in the warehouse. She walked faster. Only a couple more shops to pass before she could turn up another street and go toward the yamen's back gate.

As she passed the entrance to a wine shop, a stout man stepped out loudly berating his companion. All at once, the fellow pivoted, as if he'd stumbled, and lunged at her. He caught Mei-hua by the arm.

She was about to twist away from his clumsy hold—using the martial arts she'd learned—when his companion pulled him back.

"You clumsy bad egg! You almost knocked this filial daughter down." He cuffed his friend on the shoulder. "We are sorry, young lady. He did not mean any harm. You can see he has had too much to drink. Please forgive his stupidity," the tall man said and cuffed his friend again.

The portly fellow took his friend's hint, and also apologized in a loud voice, his tones slurred.

Mei-hua fleetingly looked around the street. Their antics were creating a scene, and, while she was glad they didn't intend any harm, she wanted to get away and out of the limelight. But the drunken duo now insisted on being her guardians.

The taller fellow looked her over through blurry eyes. "You're in mourning and all alone on the street. That's not safe." He staggered slightly, regained his balance, and looked around. "Which way is your home? We'll escort you."

Their show of concern and consideration was almost worse than if they attacked her. She could have fought off their attack, but how was she to turn away their offer to help? She would be a target walking down the street with these two drunken oafs at her side.

"That won't be necessary," a familiar voice said from behind her.

Mei-hua's heart stopped; she couldn't breathe.

The two men looked up at the speaker and their eyes grew round. "No problem." "We were trying to help." "She was alone." "We were...."

"You may leave," the young voice said sternly. Without pausing, the men quickly shuffled away, leaning onto each other for support.

Mei-hua bit her lip and turned around. Soldier Guo stood scowling at her.

"Are you trying to get hurt? What's your problem?" he asked.

"I don't have a problem," she said, but she thought, *you're my problem.*

He looked her over. "Then what are you doing walking around alone on a public street in a mourning outfit? What happened?"

He was seething; she could see complete annoyance flash in his ink-black eyes. He didn't wait for her to respond. He went on, "Guei-lung came back to court without you, saying you'd been kidnapped. Judge Hsu has soldiers out everywhere looking for you."

He stepped closer to her. "You saw me back there and ran away. Why?"

She unconsciously stepped back and was almost immediately sorry she had. She didn't want him to think she was afraid of him. She straightened her shoulders and looked him directly in the eyes. "You know the answer to that as well as I do," she snapped.

A look of confusion momentarily crossed his face. "I don't know what you mean," he said.

She was tired of his lying, of pretending to guard her when he was spying on her, and of collaborating with her enemy. "Do you seriously think we don't know about you and why you're really at Judge Hsu's court?"

He pressed his lips into a hard line and stared at her. Finally, he said, "Ah, I see."

He stepped forward again. This time she held her ground.

He drew his eyebrows together; his face reflected both pain and remorse. "Mei-hua, it's not what you think. My situation is not easy, but I'm not here to hurt you. I promise. Trust me. I'd never hurt you."

Conflicted, she glanced away. *Trust me.* She wanted to trust him, but how could she? He was her father's enemy.

He reached out and adjusted her mugwort hairpin. The pressure of his hand on her hair made her tremble. At the same time, she furtively glanced around. Had anyone noticed his familiar—too familiar—gesture? A cataclysm of emotions whirled through her. She took in a steadying deep breath.

"What do you intend to do now?" she asked, trying to keep her voice neutral.

"Escort you back to Judge Hsu. He's very concerned about you. He believes you were kidnapped. And, of course, Madam Wu is beside herself with worry."

Mei-hua didn't respond. Guilt now piled on to her other emotions. Madam Wu. This kidnapping attempt will only add to her list of reasons to be anxious about Mei-hua and, she thought ruefully, give her yet another reason to demand Mei-hua remain within the confines of the women's quarters. And who could blame her?

"Well?" Guo said.

She looked up at him not understanding.

"Are you ready to go back?"

She nodded and they walked down the street together, the merriment of the surging throng around them a foil against her churning emotions.

*****

Her entrance created a great deal of excitement. News of her return shot through the yamen in record time. Madam Wu wanted her to come into the women's quarters immediately. She needed to be taken care of—given a bath, fed, and allowed to rest—after telling Madam Wu, Ping-an, and the others her story, of course. However, the judge insisted she come to his office first.

As soon as she and Solder Guo arrived at his door, a guard immediately admitted them.

The judge sat upright behind his desk, his attention aimed at the two.

"Zhang Mei-hua, come and sit. Sit." He pointed toward a chair near his desk and she obeyed, placing herself on the seat's edge. Soldier Guo took up his position on the side of the judge's desk. He remained standing, stiff and at attention.

"Good work, Guo," he said and nodded toward the young soldier.

"Thank you, Sir. I found her in the street two blocks from here. She was returning home."

Mei-hua threw him a grateful glance. She was glad he didn't mention the drunks. She was in enough trouble.

"Now tell me what happened to you from the time you were kidnapped. My secretary will take notes," Hsu said. There was no smile, no softening of his tone. He was on duty and all seriousness.

She took a deep breath. "I had stopped on our way home to buy Duanwu treats for the maids. I was returning to the carriage with Lotus Blossom when one of Ching Da's henchmen grabbed me and dragged me into a nearby shop. When I struggled to get away, someone knocked me out. While I was unconscious, they put this mourning robe on me." She looked down at the white garment. "I think it was supposed to hide my clothing."

Judge Hsu nodded and waited for her to continue.

"Then they carried me out into the streets and to the warehouse Guei-lung and I had seen Ching Da in earlier. The one with the goods for the tea-horse trade, where they were building a dragon boat."

Judge Hsu tapped his chin as he thought about this news.

"They kept me in a large wooden box, which had spaces between its slats. I was able to observe much of what went on in the warehouse."

"So, Ching Da was behind your kidnapping. We expected this and, even though we couldn't prove it at the time, I sent out police to arrest him and his gang on other charges. I've just received word he's in custody."

At Mei-hua's surprised look, he added with a satisfied nod, "It wasn't hard to find something to pin on him. He's left a wide path of illegal activity." The judge tugged at his beard once more.

"Ching Da was about to leave the warehouse when my soldiers arrived and put him in chains. But," he examined Mei-hua closely, "you weren't in your prison when the soldiers arrived. They had found one mugwort sandal, that's all. What happened? How did you escape?"

"The men in the warehouse had all placed bets on the dragon boat they built. So when the races began, they left the warehouse en masse—except my guard. He stayed, but still couldn't resist the excitement of the race. When the boats began to pass by on the river, he left my cage to watch.

"I was able to use my hairpin," she touched her mugwort pin with its tiger figure, "to push the bolt out of place. Unfortunately, when I opened the warehouse door and was about to escape, there was Ching Da. He almost caught me again. I managed to get past him and run down the wharf and toward the yamen and home. That's when Soldier Guo caught—found—me."

"Ah, my soldiers must have arrived just after you escaped. If only they had gotten there earlier. Still, your testimony will help convict Ching Da of stealing and kidnapping."

Hsu stroked his beard. "Nevertheless, this case appears too complicated and involves too many people with a long reach into the national bureaucracy for such a minor criminal. There must be another mind behind it all."

"Sir, I believe I know who it is."

Hsu nodded. "Don't be afraid to speak. Tell me what you think."

"When I was in the cage, a man Ching Da called "Boss" came to see what progress the men were making. He has to be the leader. I believe he was also the person who ordered my kidnapping. He planned to use me to force my father to cover up an investigation he was carrying out. The boss didn't say it, but it seems most logical that the criminal activity involved the tea-horse trade and its network of thieves."

Judge Hsu nodded. "Very good. Very good. Did you see him? Could you identify him? Did you find out his name?"

"He made no attempt to hide. He had me pulled out of the cage and talked to me about my father."

"It was foolish of him to let you see his face. He could have left all interactions with you to Ching Da," Hsu said.

"He wasn't concerned about my seeing him because, as I heard him tell Ching Da, he wanted me killed. He never intended to allow me to return home."

Magistrate Hsu gave a resounding slap on the desk, his eyes blazed. "He'll regret that intent," he muttered angrily.

"And his name?" the judge asked again.

"I don't know. They called him the Boss."

The judge nodded and took up a sheet of paper. "I have a name here of a local Changsha man. His family is an old and well connected one. He is a merchant and has businesses in several cities, including Hangzhou. He's a part of the tea-horse trade which starts here, goes through Changsha, and then out to the west. In spite of your father's suspicions, however, he still hasn't been able to find strong enough evidence against him. He's been quite clever."

Hsu held the sheet in his fingers. "Even with the arrest of Ching Da, until we have the gang's boss you are still in danger, as is your father."

Mei-hua closed her eyes. Would this never end?

"What's his name?" she asked.

"Gu Long-lai."

She started. "Gu Long-lai?"

"Does that name mean something to you?"

"Yes, but I didn't recognize it as his name at the time," she said. "When I was in the cage, the boss came in at the same time as the workers started moving the great dragon boat. They shouted 'Look around, the dragon is coming,' and I thought they were warning people to be careful. They *were* warning people to be careful, but it was because their boss, Gu Long-lai, had entered the building."

"Yes, that's what his name would mean, but are you sure? You do not want to make a mistake on such an important point," the judge cautioned her.

Mei-hua shook her head excitedly. "They were shouting his name and I thought they were talking about the dragon boat."

"You have provided the essential missing key. I will send a message along with a copy of your report to your father immediately. He can now rest assured that you're safe. He'll be able to prosecute his case against Gu."

"What about Gu, though? I don't know where he went. He didn't say. He could easily get away," Mei-hua frowned.

The judge gave a grim smile. "No problem. When we learned he was in Hangzhou, we put a trace on him. My men alerted me just before you came in that he is at the river. The dragon boat you saw being built in the warehouse was his. It won the race this afternoon. Gu was at the races all day and apparently didn't know anything about your escape. He's just been seen at the winner's line, celebrating with his crew. I am having him brought in now before he finds out about you and that his plans have all just gone up in smoke."

Relief flooded through Mei-hua. Her nightmare was finally over. Her family was safe.

A boot scraped against wood, drawing her attention away from the judge and to Soldier Guo, who stood nearby, listening. Her mind raced. Did this mean he wasn't involved? Or could Gu have been working for Lord Chiu?

She looked up at Judge Hsu. How could she discuss this with him when Soldier Guo was in the room? She gulped. She had no choice.

"Sir?" she started.

"Yes?"

She tugged her head in Guo's direction. "What about...? What about...?" she stuttered, unable to quite say the words.

Hsu looked from her to Guo and back.

"Ah, yes. Another lose end." And this time a pleased smile slide across his lips.

"First, you may find it interesting to know that Solder Guo's adopted father, Lord Chiu, is Uyghur."

Now Mei-hua was only more confused. What did the ethnicity of the man trying to harm them mean to her and her father?

Chapter 20

"YES, WE WERE CORRECT in our early assessment. Young Guo here was acting as a spy for his father. And that included not only spying on you but ingratiating himself with the local criminals in order to be able to keep an eye on their activities as well. That's why you saw him with Ching Da." He nodded in satisfaction. "Yes, he certainly will go far in a career as a spy."

Mei-hua unconsciously stiffened and stared at Soldier Guo.

Judge Hsu quickly continued, "But for other reasons than we imagined." He settled back in his chair and waited as his assistant brought tea for them. After making sure she had a cup, the judge took his and held it before him. "Since the Uyghur connection is another key to understanding the puzzle of Lord Chiu, his adopted son, and your father, we'll begin with it.

"As you may know by now, Lord Chiu is directly under the Managing Grand Eunuch in the Ceremonial Directorate. And, therefore, he has quite a network of secret service agents, which he oversees for our Esteemed Emperor. It is one of the most important posts in the Imperial government. He has easy contact with the Emperor and is a trusted confidant. However, before Lord Chiu became such an exulted person, he had a very different life." He waved a hand at Mei-hua's tea cup. "Drink your tea. This story will take a while." He grinned and continued.

"During the Yuan Dynasty, the bureaucracy of the country was mostly filled with Han literati. Men who were highly educated and had passed through three levels of civil service examinations. However, to protect their dynasty and their own interests, the Yuan Dynasty Emperors never allowed the Han to learn Mongolian. Language is power, and they didn't want the Han Chinese to hold that power. At the same time, all official documents and pronouncements had to be written in both Mongolian and Chinese.

"There needed to be an intermediary, an interface between these two ethnic and power groups. The Uyghur, who spoke both languages but were neither Mongolian nor Han, filled this role."

Mei-hua nodded. She was well aware of the role played by her mother's people during the last dynasty.

"A few years before the Hongwu Emperor officially established the Ming Dynasty, there was a great battle in the northern part of the country. The residing Uyghur, who worked for the Yuan Emperor and his family, were considered to be spoils of war and were taken as slaves. Lord Chiu was one of them. He was serving the Emperor—as many of his fellow Uyghur did—as a translator between the ruling foreign Mongols and the Han Chinese majority in their empire."

Judge Hsu took a sip of his tea and placed it back on the highly polished table. He observed Mei-hua closely. "When Lord Chiu was a student, he'd studied under Amir al-Din."

Mei-hua's eyes widened and she flashed a brief look at Guo.

"That's right. Your mother's father. Your grandfather was celebrated for his brilliance and education among both the Uyghur and the Han. He'd been an intermediary for the Mongol rulers. When he retired, he returned to his home in the west and taught the occasional student. They were exceptional young men that he thought showed great promise. Lord Chiu was one of them. And, being among the brightest, he was already working for the Mongol royalty as quite a young man."

The Judge stopped and seemed to study his tea, as if there was something wrong with it. He exhaled noisily and continued, "After the battle, the 'spoils of war' were taken away as slaves. Lord Chiu's intellectual abilities were quickly established and he was taken into the Ming court. However, as a male he could easily become a threat to the Emperor. As he gained power and wealth working in the government, he would place his family's interest over the Emperor's best interests. And then there was always the threat he would pose to the Emperor if he had access to any of the women in the royal family. There was one solution, which the Emperor didn't fail to use.

"Lord Chiu was made into a eunuch. As such, he was no longer a potential threat to the Emperor. Now he was a trustworthy, loyal servant."

Mei-hua gasped. What a cruel fate for someone who had begun life with such promise.

"Once Lord Chiu had his manhood taken from him, the Emperor brought him into his inner circle of trusted servants."

"Why does the Emperor need a translator?" Mei-hua asked.

"Good question. He doesn't. Lord Chiu has been most involved in creating a secret service of sorts for the Emperor."

"A spy network," she said, knitting her brows.

He grinned. "The Emperor Hongwu must know what's really happening in his country. Officials may lie to make themselves look good or to hide their stealing from the government; others may lie because they are building a revolution against the government. How would he know?"

"Meaning," Mei-hua interjected, "Soldier Guo is a spy working for his uncle, Lord Chiu." She stared hard at Guo. He remained at attention; his handsome face unreadable and his sight on the middle-distance. Focusing on nothing, yet always alert. "But what has this to do with my father?"

"And that's where the story gets interesting," Hsu said. "Remember, your grandfather was Lord Chiu's teacher and that is one of the strongest relationships a man can have. A student's bond with his teacher is ironclad. His teacher is like a father to him and the student owes him the loyalty, obedience, and respect he would owe a father.

"Lord Chiu's spies were looking into tea-horse trade shipments that appeared to be losing as much as thirty to forty percent of their product at times. Some loss was to be expected, but this was too much. Although his initial investigation into the loss of goods was confidential, he'd already begun hearing rumors about your father. On the one side, there was suspicion he was the criminal leader. Lord Chiu's spies had heard rumors about your father, claiming he was a snake in the grass, one who spoke quiet hate against the Honorable Emperor and his new dynasty. As proof of your father's disloyalty, they pointed to his marrying a foreigner, a Uyghur woman. They claimed that such a marriage proved your father wanted a return to the Yuan Dynasty."

Mei-hua sprang forward to defend her family. Judge Hsu stopped her with a raised hand.

"Lord Chiu had to determine what was true. Our Honorable Emperor is searching out traitors and would-be traitors relentlessly and with a vengeance. Even the hint of any such rumor reaching our Esteemed Emperor could destroy a man and his family.

"In his investigation, Lord Chiu discovered your father had indeed married a Uyghur woman—the daughter of his honored teacher Amir al-Din and that she'd had a daughter: you."

Mei-hua was overwhelmed by all this information and the intertwined history of her family and Soldier Guo's. Still, there was so much more to know. After digesting this news, she finally asked, "But how did he find me here, with you? I didn't even know your name."

"This may not make you feel comfortable, but Lord Chiu already had spies within your father's court and his household. One of the servants noticed your Old Nanny worriedly packing things. She reported it to her contact and Lord Chiu knew about your leaving almost before you did."

"Well, if he was so clever, why did he let my Nanny and Old Lin get murdered and let me get kidnapped and sold as an indentured servant?" she asked angrily.

He looked at her with sympathy. "A spy's task is to observe and report, not to interfere. However, you'll be pleased to know," he grinned at her, "they reported back to Lord Chiu that you were exceptionally able for a girl."

She grimaced at the compliment. "And what about Nanny and Old Lin? Don't their lives count for anything?"

"I'll get to that. Let me continue."

Mei-hua tried to control her impatience. "Yes, sir."

"It's because they knew you were here that they sent Soldier Guo. Not, as we thought, to spy on you—they already had a bevy of spies watching you and your father—but to protect you from whomever was behind the tea-horse trade stealing."

Again, Mei-hua started. Protect her? He was here to protect her, not spy on her or to hurt her? She stared up at Guo again. She suspected she saw his black eyes twinkling, although his face remained immobile. Just as she was about to turn her attention back to Judge Hsu, Guo looked over at her and held her gaze. She felt a rush of happiness. Heat rose from her neck and into her cheeks. She hoped she wasn't blushing, but her face burned with pleasure. Then she looked away. A note of sadness began to replace her short-lived delight at this news. She was acutely aware that it was unlikely their paths would ever cross again—since he was a soldier and she a magistrate's daughter. She sighed. No one could know the future or their fate.

Mei-hua pulled her attention back to Judge Hsu. "And what about my Nanny, Old Lin, and the boy, young Chen? You said you were going to tell me about them."

"They were recently found still recuperating in a remote temple. Both of your servants are elderly and had received serious head injuries from the bandits who kidnapped you. The monks didn't know if they would survive. Old Lin recovered first and sent the family's young servant to your father, letting him know they were alive and that you'd been captured by bandits. Of course, by this time, your father knew you'd been captured, but he was delighted to discover that they'd been in the healing hands of the temple monks."

She clapped her hands in spontaneous delight. He smiled.

"It's time for you to join your father, Mei-hua. It's safe. You are going home."

In a paroxysm of joy, she jumped up from her chair, laughing.

"You are so unemotional," he joked.

She looked at him, her face lit with happiness. She bowed deeply. After so many months of hiding, of not knowing who she could trust or who of her loved ones were alive or dead, she finally, truly, believed she and her family were safe.

"Thank you so much, Uncle," she said.

He smiled. "Yes, you'll always be my niece. Your father and I have a lifelong bond; we are like brothers." He rested a hand on the desk. "I'm afraid my son and daughter may not be as delighted as you are. They will miss you. But you must return often and visit. We are family."

Mei-hua took in a full, filling, breath. "We are family."

The End

Author's Note: Mei-hua's World

In **Trapped,** the character Lord Chen is not a real, historical person. However, in many ways he represents the kind of person who could have lived during this time and in these circumstances. He was a eunuch who held a high position within the Ming Dynasty's (1368-1644) governmental administration. Eunuchs were particularly influential during the Ming Dynasty, since they were considered a power counter balance to the literati-- government officials who filled most of the national bureaucracy.

Eunuchs

Eunuchs had the potential for great power through direct access to the Emperor. They were trusted male servants used in the imperial palaces at least since the Han Dynasty (206 BC- 220 AD). Their numbers and influence grew through the centuries. By the Ming Dynasty, it has been estimated that there were tens of thousands of eunuchs working in the Imperial palaces. They not only performed services for the Emperor, both personal as servants and governmental as officials, but they also were the only men allowed contact with the Emperor's wives and concubines.

What is a eunuch? Eunuchs are surgically castrated men and boys. People became eunuchs because they either chose or were chosen to work in the imperial palaces. Once the decision was made, the boy or man would go to a surgeon who specialized in this area. Needless to say, this was a dangerous operation and people sometimes died due to excessive bleeding or other complications.

Why become a eunuch? There were several reasons boys and men became eunuchs:

• Being a eunuch was considered by some talented men, who had few other opportunities, to be an alternative path to wealth and power. Brilliant men who were not castrated—like Judge Hsu—could also reach high office after years of rigorous study and passing three major national examinations. However, they would never have the intimate relationship with the Emperor that was available to the non-threatening eunuch of the same level of training and skill.

• At minimum, at a time when there were few options for the very poor, making a son a eunuch almost guaranteed him at least a decent livelihood—and the possibility, if he was clever, of much, much more.

• Castration was sometimes used against captured enemies in the time of war. Many other cultures also followed this practice, not just the Chinese or during the Ming Dynasty.

• If the Emperor wanted a particular person castrated, that was considered the ruler's right. There was no alternative and the person chosen had no choice.

• The Emperor had two main reasons for wanting only eunuchs in his private spaces throughout his palaces.

o From the Emperor's perspective, a man who could not have male offspring was less of a threat to him and his dynasty. A eunuch could not set up a new dynasty since he'd have no sons to succeed him. All of the eunuch's power and influence would be dependent on the current Emperor's success in holding power. In the Mei-hua trilogy, Lord Chiu adopts Soldier Guo as his son, but in reality, such a relationship would probably have been unheard of at the time. I put this in the stories to highlight the importance of filial piety. The loyalty Guo exhibits towards Lord Chiu is consistent with the expected behavior of all children towards their parents at that time. Filial piety was a virtue that overrode everything else. Even the laws were written to not only encourage supreme loyalty to your ancestors, your father, and all older males in your paternal line, but to demand it. The Emperor would not have wanted such divided loyalty amongst those with the most intimate access to him when he was at his most vulnerable.

o An Emperor could have over a hundred concubines in addition to many wives. He did not want an unknown male to become physically involved with any of them and perhaps impregnate one of the women. In ancient China, there was no way of telling if the baby was the Emperor's child and a rightful heir to the throne or not. The best way of deterring such a disaster was to ensure that all men who came in contact with any of the palace women were unable to reproduce. Drastic as it was, this was their way of ensuring the Emperor's rightful lineage.

What did eunuchs do in the Ming government? Over the centuries, China developed a system of government that was based on a meritocracy. A meritocracy is where people achieve their positions based on their abilities and talents, not by birth, such as being a member of a noble family. In this way, the Emperor could rule his country through the best and brightest minds. These men (for this was only for males) occupied positions throughout the governmental system, from the magistrate at the local level to the very highest positions in the country. By the Ming Dynasty, a three tier examination system had become the established route to becoming a part of the national bureaucracy. To be appointed to the lowest office, district magistrate, a man had to have passed through the three examinations at the highest level. The Emperor or his administration often only assigned a position to those passing in the top 1%. The competition was tough and ambitious young men studied intensely to pass the examinations. Because there was no national education system, this required the use of private tutors hired by the families or clans themselves.

With the potential for wealth, status, and power being so great, those men who didn't pass their examinations the first time would take them again and again, spending their lives trying to move up the examination ladder. However, there were a couple of alternative routes to achieving powerful positions from which a man and his birth family could gain great wealth. As noted above, becoming a eunuch was one. Bright, ambitious men, who came from poor families and didn't have the advantage of a formal education, could become as powerful as, or even more powerful than, their non-eunuch counterparts. This was particularly true during the early Ming Dynasty.

Emperor Hongwu needed a well-educated, ever-ready pool of men to fill his bureaucracy; however, he didn't trust these men. He came from a poor farmer's family himself and viewed the educated elite with suspicion. On the other hand, all around him there were eunuchs whose sole goal in life was to serve him and whose own well-being was dependent upon his. These were men he could trust—as far as he could trust anyone. As a result, he used the eunuchs in sensitive positions, and even set them up in a network which he spread throughout the country especially to spy on his officials. Their job was to ferret out any hint of treasonous thought or behavior, as well as to make sure the various government officials were not cheating the government or stealing from it. In other words, they were his secret police and his spies. By 1380, the Emperor used eunuchs for carrying out massive political purges as well as surveillance of his officials. Unfortunately, in such a situation, it was quite easy for the unscrupulous to use the trust the Emperor had in them for their own benefit and to destroy their own enemies along with the Emperor's possible enemies.

Battle in 1368 between Mongols and Han Chinese

In the summer of 1368, Ming forces captured Beijing, the center of the Mongol rule over China, thus bringing an end to the Yuan Dynasty after only ninety years of dominating the country. At least six Mongol princes, their families, and their servants—mostly eunuchs—were captured and held hostage. This was followed in 1371 by the capture of the grandson and potential heir of the last Emperor of the Yuan Dynasty, as well as hundreds of the Emperor's extended family members, eunuchs, and officials.

Tea-horse Trade

The most important job of the military was to keep the country safe from invaders. In Ming China, invaders meant people from the west and north. To protect the country, many soldiers were stationed along the Great Wall in the north, but soldiers also had to be ready to battle across the great sweep of open areas to the northwest and west. In order to cover such an enormous territory, the military required a great, effective cavalry, which in turn needed strong, dependable horses. A trade system built around the acquisition of such horses had already begun at the very beginning of the Ming Dynasty, for the best mounts came from territories in the west (including today's Tibet) and north. The first documented incident of tea-horse trading took place in 1375. At that time, the Grand Eunuch Zhao Chen traded tea and textiles from China for horses from Shaanxi.

Although the ideas and mechanisms of the trade were in place by the date of our story, the licensing of merchants and horse traders weren't actually formalized until a few years after 1380. Illegal activities—tea smuggling and illegal trading of other goods—became an immediate problem, which was difficult to control.

Procuring horses for the cavalry was under the jurisdiction of eunuchs. While non-eunuchs carried out the logistics of the tea-for-horse transactions, the eunuchs were ultimately responsible. Losses due to theft or other abuses were their problem.

Ethnicity and Eunuchs in Ming China

Most eunuchs were Han Chinese; however, many came from different ethnic groups. These non-Han were often brought in as the spoils of war and as tribute for the Emperor from neighboring states.

The relationship between Han and non-Han peoples was complex and varied with time, place, and individuals. However, generally speaking, although non-Han peoples were all considered to be barbarians of one level or another, once they accepted the Chinese world-view and system of moral behavior—which was based on Confucianism as a universal principal—they were able to participate in the wealth and power of China. This mutual acceptance of sinification was desirable for many reasons. All peoples benefited, including the Chinese themselves, due not only to the importance of trade and national security, but also because there were many, many different ethnic groups living within China's borders and because their cities were quite cosmopolitan.

As is typical in any long term interaction, what happened in China may be considered a synthesis between the Han and their many neighbors as well as those non-Han within their borders. But the ancient Chinese preferred to see it as a sinification—a change of the non-Han to Han morals, values, and behaviors—rather than a synthesis. That is, the non-Han acculturated to the dominant Han Chinese culture. The highly sinicized Chuang, who lived largely in the present province of western Kwangsi, are a good example. At one time in China's history, a member of the Chuang ethnic group served as a tutor to the Emperor. Thus, barbarians could become Chinese if they totally assimilated Chinese culture—education, clothing, manners, family systems, ethnics, etc.

As noted above, when Ming forces took over a palace area they captured hundreds of eunuchs. This is how many northern Mongolians became a part of the system. The Mongolian eunuchs were already well trained in serving the ruling elite and were, therefore, valuable. Plus, castration was often used as a punishment for the losers in battle. Both of these sources provided a ready supply of servants.

From the beginning of the Ming Dynasty, states from the southeast and the east wanted to set up good relations with their powerful neighbor. These territories established foreign embassies and sent tributary missions to the Emperor. This was another source of multiethnic eunuchs, since eunuchs from their own countries were included in the tributary missions. Over time, such tributes were sent from places as diverse as Korea, Japan, Annam (the northern part of present day Vietnam), Cambodia, Siam, Borneo and the Malayan peninsula. Most likely due to a similarity in writing script and geographic proximity, Korea and Annam sent the most eunuchs. For example, in 1383 the king of Annam sent a mission to the Ming court which included 25 castrated boys. Some of these foreign eunuchs eventually enjoyed a degree of power within the Ming court along with the native, Han Chinese eunuchs.

References

Ebrey, Patricia Buckley. **Chinese Civilization**, The Free Press: New York. 263:1993, second edition.

Ebrey, Patricia Buckley. **China, Cambridge Illustrated History**, Cambridge University Press: New York, 2004.

Elvin, Mark. **The Pattern of the Chinese Past**, Stanford University Press: Stanford, CA, 1973.

Fu, Yingying et al. **Anecdotes about the Duanwu Festival**. Shanghai Foreign Language Education Press: Shanghai, 2008

Tsai, Shih-shan Henry. **The Eunuchs in the Ming Dynasty**, State University of New York Press: Albany, New York, 4:1996.

I hope you enjoyed
your Mei-hua adventure.

To discover more stories
about ancient China visit
padevoe.com.

www.ingramcontent.com/pod-product-compliance
Lightning Source LLC
Chambersburg PA
CBHW050535190726
48284CB00003B/1081